Across the Street

Georges Simenon

Across the Street

Translated from the French by John Petrie

A Helen and Kurt Wolff Book

Harcourt Brace Jovanovich, Publishers

New York   San Diego   London

First published in England in 1954 by Routledge & Kegan Paul Ltd.
This is a translation of *La Fenêtre des Rouet*, 1945.

Library of Congress Cataloging-in-Publication Data
Simenon, Georges, 1903–1989
[Fenêtre des Rouet. English]
Across the street/Georges Simenon; translated
from the French by John Petrie.—1st ed.
p.   cm.
Translation of: La Fenêtre des Rouet.
Originally published: London: Routledge & Kegan, 1954.
ISBN 0-15-103266-1
"A Helen and Kurt Wolff book."
I. Title.
PQ2637.I53F4313   1992
843'.912—dc20   92-7218

Printed in the United States of America
First United States edition
A B C D E

Part One

— *1* —

The ringing of a cheap alarm clock broke out beyond the wall. Dominique jumped as though she were the one the interminable ringing was intended to rouse at three o'clock in the afternoon. A feeling of shame. Why? The common clatter brought back to her nothing but distressing, sordid memories of illness, of tending the sick at midnight or at dawn. But she had not been asleep, she had not even dozed off. Not for a second had her hand stopped plying her needle. Indeed, just before, she had been like a circus horse, forgotten at rehearsal, trotting round and round; then pulling up short, with a shudder, on hearing a voice.

How could the people in the next room—there behind the brown door, almost on top of her—how could they endure that insolent din? They had merely to stretch out an arm, without opening an eye, and fumble a way to the clock vibrating on the table. Yet they did not: they did not move. They were naked, she knew, flesh against flesh, entwined, with sweat glistening on their skin, and their hair sticking to their temples. They were happily at home in their warmth, in their atmosphere of animal instinct. Somebody was moving, at last, somebody was stretching; eyelids blinked. There was a sleepy voice. It was the woman, mechanically seeking the man's body beside her own and stammering:

"Albert . . ."

Dominique's fingers had not stopped. Her head had remained bent over the dress she was darning under the sleeve, where all her dresses wore out, especially in summer, because she perspired so much.

She had been sewing for two hours, with tiny stitches, rebuilding a fabric as fine as that of the original white material with a mauve pattern; and, now that her tenants' alarm clock had made her jump, she could not have said what she had been thinking about during those two hours. It was hot. Never had the air felt so heavy. In the afternoon, the sun beat full on this side of Rue du Faubourg Saint-Honoré. Dominique had closed her shutters, but not quite joined the two halves. She had left a vertical gap a few inches wide, giving her a view of the buildings opposite; the molten sunlight poured through it and, on either side, gleamed through the narrower horizontal gaps between the slats.

After a time this pattern of light, from which sprang burning heat, etched itself on the eyes and the brain. A sudden glance elsewhere projected it instantaneously on the brown door, the wall, or the floor.

Buses passed every two minutes. They could be felt, like enormous waves breaking in the canyon of the street. There was something vicious in their brutality, particularly those climbing toward the Place des Ternes, as, with a sudden grinding of gears, they tackled the steepening gradient in front of her home. Dominique was used to them, but it was the same as with the rays of the sun: she felt them in spite of herself, and the noise penetrated her brain, leaving a humming aftermath. Surely the alarm next door had stopped? Yet she thought she heard it still. Perhaps the air was so heavy that it retained the imprint of sounds the way mud retains the track of passing feet.

She could not see the sidewalk opposite. She got a view of it only when she stood up. Yet certain images persisted. For example, the lemon-yellow front of the dairy, the name, in green, over the window—AUDEBAL —the fruits and vegetables, the baskets on the sidewalk. And from time to time—despite the noises of the city, the blasts of the policeman's whistle at the Haussmann crossing, the horns of taxis, the bells of Saint-Philippe-du-Roule—a small familiar noise reached her, distinct from the others, the high-pitched bell of the dairy.

She was hot, although almost naked. She had never before done what she had done today. She had taken off her dress to mend it and had not put on another. She had remained in her slip. She was worried about it, a little ashamed. Two or three times she had nearly got up to put something on, especially when her glance fell on herself, when she felt the quivering of her breasts, which she could see, very white, very delicate, in the opening of her slip. Another sensation was strange, almost sexual—the beads of perspiration breaking through her skin at almost equal intervals. It seemed to take a very long time. Impatience seized her before, at last, the warm drop that had sprung out under an armpit trickled slowly down her side.

"Not now, Albert . . ."

A childish voice. Lina, in the room next door, was

not yet twenty-two. She was a plump doll, rather soft, with reddish hair and russet lights playing over her white flesh. Her voice was soft too, padded with animal well-being. Dominique blushed and snapped her thread with the sharp action of all seamstresses. She didn't want to hear any more. She knew it, she was not mistaken—a scratching noise was already heralding the phonograph record they played every time they "did it."

And they had not closed the shutters. They thought they were out of sight because the bed was at the far end of the room, where the sun did not reach, and because in this month of August most of the buildings opposite were empty. But Dominique knew well enough that old Augustine, up there in one of the attics, was watching them.

At three o'clock in the afternoon! These young people of the 1930s slept no matter when, they lived no matter how; and the first thing they did when they got home was to undress. They were not embarrassed, and Dominique was the one who dared not cross the common living room, a room she had not rented to them but which they had to cross to get to the bathroom. Two or three times she had met Albert there quite naked, with a towel carelessly knotted around his middle.

They always played the same record, a tango they must have heard on some unforgettable occasion. Worse, there was a detail that made their presence still more palpable, so much so that their very movements seemed almost visible: when the record had finished, when only the scratching of the needle was to be heard, there was a kind of hesitancy, lasting quite long, a terrible silence, and it was nearly always Lina's voice that stammered:

6

"The record . . ."

The phonograph was close by the bed; through the whispering and laughter, the movements the man made in order to reach it could be visualized.

He loved her. He loved her like an animal. He spent his life loving her, and he would do so in front of anybody. When they went out shortly after, they still felt the need, even in the street, to press close against each other.

The dress was darned. Yet it looked all the poorer, poorer for having been so well darned, with such tiny stitches. The fabric had no substance left after so many washings and ironings. How many now? The mauve was for half-mourning. That meant a year after her father's death: four summers she had been wearing that dress, washing it at six in the morning so it would be dried and ironed by the time she had to go and do her shopping.

She raised her head. Yes, old Augustine was at her post, her elbows on the sill of her attic window, full of indignation as she gazed down into the next room. For a second, now that she was on her feet, Dominique was tempted to take a couple of paces, to bend down, to look through the keyhole. She had done that sometimes.

Ten past three. She would put her dress on again. Then she would darn the stockings lying in the brown wickerwork basket, a basket that dated from the time of her grandmother, which had always contained stockings waiting to be darned. You might think they were always the same and that you could darn for century after century without emptying it.

A reflection in the big rectangular mirror of the wardrobe, and suddenly Dominique, her nostrils pinched, let slip one shoulder strap, then the other, as though by accident, and her burning eyes gazed at the mirror and the image, oh so white, of her breasts.

So white! It had never occurred to her before to make a comparison, since she had never had the opportunity to look at the naked body of another woman. Now, she had seen Lina, who was golden and covered with an invisible down that caught the light. But Lina at almost twenty-two was still unformed: her shoulders were rounded and each marked with a dimple; she was cast in one piece, with no figure, her waist as full as her hips. Her breasts, however, were full, and when she lay down, they seemed to sprawl on her with all their weight.

Hesitantly, as though she might be caught, Dominique grasped her small, firm, pointed breasts, which had remained exactly the same as when she was sixteen. Her skin was finer than that of the finest fruit, with gleams of ivory in some hollows and fleeting blue tinges of veins in others. In three months she would be forty, she would be old; people must speak of her as an old maid already, and yet she knew that she had the body of a child, that she was young and fresh from head to foot, and to the very depths of her heart.

For a second she clasped her breasts as though they were the flesh of a stranger, turning her eyes away from the thin white face in the mirror. It was thinner than it used to be, which made the nose seem even longer and more crooked. A fraction of an inch that had perhaps altered her whole character, had made her timid, sensitive, gloomy.

They turned the phonograph on again. In a few moments there would be sounds of coming and going, and the man would sing. He nearly always sang afterward. Then he would open the bathroom door noisily, and his voice would come from farther away. Everything was audible. Dominique had not wanted to take in a couple. Albert Caille was alone when he arrived, a thin young man with burning eyes, and with such sincerity in his face and, at the same time, such a hunger for life that it was impossible to refuse him.

He had cheated. He had not admitted to her that he was engaged and would be getting married shortly. When he announced it, he had put on a suppliant look, whose effects he knew well.

"You'll see . . . it will be exactly the same. . . . We'll live like bachelors, my wife and I. . . . We'll have our meals at a restaurant. . . ."

Dominique was embarrassed at her nakedness, and she pulled up her shoulder straps; her head disappeared for an instant in the dress. She pulled it down over her hips and made sure, before she sat down again, that nothing was out of place in the room, that everything was tidy.

A car horn she recognized. She had no need to lean out and look. She knew it was Madame Rouet's little open car. She had seen her leave after lunch, about two o'clock. She was wearing a white outfit with a scarf of almond-green organdy, a hat to match, and shoes and bag of the same green. Antoinette Rouet would never leave home in an outfit with a single jarring detail.

And why? For whom? Where had she been, alone at the wheel of her car, which would now be left standing for hours at the curb?

Three-thirty. She was late. Old Madame Rouet must be furious. Dominique could see her. She had only to raise her eyes. On the other side of the street they did not get the afternoon sun, so they did not close the shutters. Today, because of the heat, all the windows were open, and everything could be seen. It was like being with other people in their room—stretch out a hand and they could be touched.

They did not know anyone was behind Dominique's shutters. On the same floor as hers, Hubert Rouet was asleep, or, to be exact, he was tossing uneasily, and had been for some minutes now, in his warm, damp bed-clothes.

He had been left alone, as he was every afternoon. The apartment was huge; it took up the whole floor. The bedroom was the last room on the left. It was op-ulent. Rouet's parents were very rich: people said they were worth many millions, but they lived like ordinary middle-class folk. There was no one to be extravagant but their daughter-in-law, Antoinette, now returning in a white outfit at the wheel of her car.

Dominique knew all about them. She had never heard the sound of their voices, which did not carry across the canyon of the street. But she saw their comings and goings from morning till night, she followed their gestures, the movements of their lips. It was a long story without words, of which she knew the smallest episodes.

When Hubert Rouet got married, his father and mother had been living on the same floor, the third, and at that time Dominique's father was still alive. He lay helpless in the next-door bedroom, the one she had since rented. Even then Dominique scarcely ever left their apartment. Her father had a little bell within reach, and he used to fly into a rage if his daughter did not come running to him at the very first tinkle.

"Where were you? What were you doing? I might die, in this house, without . . ."

Albert Caille could be heard splashing about in the bathroom. Luckily she had put an old piece of linoleum there: otherwise the floor would long since have rotted.

Old Madame Rouet was sitting at her window. She was immediately over her son's head, for, when he married, his parents had given the apartment to him and had moved up one floor. The building belonged to them, and a good part of the street, too.

Sometimes his mother, who had bad legs, would listen. She could be seen listening, wondering whether her son was calling. Sometimes she grasped a bellpull that communicated with the kitchen on the floor below. Dominique could not see this kitchen, which looked out on the rear of the building, but she could count the seconds, and she was sure soon to see the young couple's maid entering the old lady's room. She guessed:

"Is your master asleep? Has your mistress not come home? Go and see whether my son needs anything. . . ."

For the past month, indeed more than a month, Hubert Rouet had been in bed. It must be serious, because the doctor came to see him every morning, a few minutes after nine, at the beginning of his rounds. Dominique recognized the horn of his car, too. She was present, after a fashion, at these calls. She knew the doctor; he was Dr. Libaud, who lived on Boulevard Haussmann and had attended her father. Their eyes had met once, and Dr. Libaud had given a slight wave to Dominique across the street.

Except for this illness, the Rouets would have been at Trouville, where they owned a villa. There was scarcely anybody in Paris. Taxis were rare. Many shops were shut, including Sutton's leather-goods shop, next to the dairy, where traveling bags were sold and where throughout the rest of the year there were trunks on each side of the entrance.

Had old Madame Rouet heard her daughter-in-law's car? All of a sudden, Rouet had turned on his bed, his mouth open as if he was trying desperately to breathe.

His attack . . .

It was the time for it. There were at least two a day, sometimes three. Once, when he had had six, they had laid ice bags on his chest throughout the day and for a good part of the night.

Unconsciously, Dominique sketched the action of picking something up: the milky vial standing on the night table in the sick man's room.

That was what he was waiting for. His eyes were open. He had never been fat, or in good condition. A drab little man, quite undistinguished. Everybody thought him badly matched to Antoinette when they were married, with great pomp, at Saint-Philippe-du-Roule. What made him even more ordinary was his colorless toothbrush mustache.

Dominique could have sworn he was looking at her, but that was impossible, because of her almost closed shutters. She could see him, but he could not see her. He was gazing into space, waiting, hoping, his fingers clutching at air. Was he going to sit up? Yes, he was sitting up, or trying to, but he could not manage it. Suddenly both his hands went to his chest, and he lay there, bent double, unable to move, his face distorted with the fear of dying.

Dominique could almost have called out some message to Antoinette Rouet, who must be on the stairs, opening the door of the apartment, taking off her hat and her green gloves:

Hurry! The attack . . .

Then a voice close at hand, coarse by reason of its familiarity, said:

"Hand me my stockings . . ."

She could not prevent herself from seeing, in her mind, Lina, naked and gorged, on the edge of the bed, still imbued with a strong male odor.

The sky was like slate. A line cut the street in two on a slant, but, on both the shady and the sunny sides the same substance, thick and viscous, filled the universe, until sounds were swallowed, and the noise of the buses reached the ears only as a far-off hum.

A door banged, the door of the bathroom; Albert Caille had finished washing. He could be heard moving briskly to and fro, whistling the tango the phonograph had been playing.

Antoinette was there. Dominique jumped, because she had seen her only by chance while looking, not at the sick man's windows, but at those next door, in a dressing room where, since her husband's illness, Antoinette had had a bed set up for herself.

She was standing close to the door between the two rooms. She had taken off her hat and gloves—Dominique was not mistaken—but why was she standing motionless, as though waiting?

It was as if the old lady upstairs had been warned by her maternal instinct. She was worried, obviously. Perhaps she was going to make a heroic effort to rise, but it was months since she had walked unaided. She was enormous. She was a tower. Her legs were thick and rigid, like columns. On the rare occasions when she went out, it took two people to hoist her into a car, and she always seemed to be threatening them with her rubber-tipped cane.

Now that there was nothing more for her to see, old Augustine had left her window. She would certainly be in the long dim hallway on her floor, onto which all the attic doors opened, on the watch for someone to pass whom she could speak to. She was capable of waiting for an hour at a time, like a monstrous spider, her hands folded across her stomach, and never once would the pasty face under the snow-white hair lose its expression of infinite gentleness.

Why did Antoinette Rouet not move? With all the strength of his eyes staring into the blazing emptiness outside, her husband was calling for help. Twice, three times, his mouth had shut, his jaws had clenched, but he had failed to gulp the mouthful of air he needed.

Dominique was as though transfixed. It seemed to her that nothing in the world could tear a movement or a sound from her. There had just come to her the certainty of real drama, of drama so unexpected, so palpable, that it was as if she herself were taking part in it at that very moment.

Rouet was condemned to die! He was going to die! Those minutes, those seconds, while the Cailles next door were cheerfully getting dressed before going out for the evening, while a bus changed gear to turn into Boulevard Haussmann, while the shop bell of the dairy tinkled—she had never been able to get used to the name Audebal, pronouncing it with embarrassment, like something incongruous—those minutes, those seconds, were the last of a man whose life she had watched for years.

14

She had never found him likable. Or maybe she had. It was complicated, and not pleasant. She had at first blamed him for letting himself be dominated by his wife, by that Antoinette who had suddenly turned the household upside down with her vitality, with her exuberant vulgarity.

Antoinette could do anything she liked. He would follow her like a sheep, and he looked rather like one. Fortunately, the old lady up above intervened!

She would ring.

"Ask madame to come upstairs. . . ."

And she would speak out, would the old lady; she would speak out in a tone very different from that of her sheep of a son. The daughter-in-law's cheeks would flush pink and red, and, back in her own apartment, she would relieve her feelings with furious gestures.

"You're being brought to heel, my girl!"

Then, the sheep had not been entirely sheeplike in Dominique's eyes. He said nothing. He never protested. Antoinette might be out all day, she might return with her car full of expensive packages, she might dress herself in outrageous clothes, but he would not protest. Yet Dominique knew that, like certain children who never take their own revenge, he had only to go upstairs to his mother's. And there he would tell all, in a level voice, his head bent. He probably used restrained language. Perhaps he even made a show of defending her.

"Ask madame to come upstairs. . . ."

Now, at this very moment, Antoinette was in the act of killing him! Dominique watched the scene. She took part in it. She knew. She knew everything. At one and the same time she was on the bed with the dying man and she was Antoinette . . .

. . . Antoinette, who, still warm with the life of the world outside, had opened the door of the apartment and suddenly felt her shoulders weighed down with the chill of the house, the silence, the familiar smells—the Rouets' apartment must smell stale, with the musty odor of medicine. . . .

The kitchen door had opened halfway.

"Ah! Madame is back. . . . I was just going to see if the master . . ."

And the maid glanced at the clock. That meant that Antoinette was late, that it was the time when the attack was due, the time for the medicine, which had to be measured out drop by drop. Fifteen—Dominique knew; she had counted them time and again.

Antoinette had taken off her hat in front of the mirror, which had reflected back to her the image of a young and elegant woman brimming over with life, and at the same moment she had heard a slight sound, her wretched husband shriveled up in his bed, his hands clasped over a heart threatening to stop. . . .

The old lady up above, that implacable tower of a mother-in-law, had rung.

"Shall I go up, madame?"

Dominique saw the maid appear.

"Has my daughter-in-law come home?"

"She has just come in, madame."

"My son has not had his attack?"

"Madame is with him."

She ought to have been! She had been, nearly. A few feet to go. And, perhaps because of that image reflected back to her by the mirror and following her like her own shadow, perhaps because of the maid's question, because of her mother-in-law's little bell—look! she has stopped.

Drops of perspiration pearled Dominique's brow. She wanted to cry out, but she could not. Did she really want to? She lived through fearful minutes, yet she experienced an unhealthy kind of pleasure. It seemed to her in a muddled sort of way that this thing taking place before her eyes was avenging her. Of what? She had no idea. She did not think. She remained there, tense, as tense as the other woman, who had laid a hand on the doorjamb and was waiting.

If the servant came down again at once, Antoinette Rouet would be obliged to go into the bedroom, to go through the routine movements: to count the drops, to pour out half a glass of water, to mix the dose, to hold up the head of the man with the colorless mustache.

But old Madame Rouet was speaking. The cushion behind her back was too high or too low. It was adjusted. The maid disappeared in the shadows of the room. She was going to go downstairs. No. She was bringing the old lady a magazine.

Rouet was on the point of death, and yet, look, he was sitting up! God knows where he had found such strength. Perhaps he had heard a slight noise on the other side of the door, for he was looking toward it. His mouth opened. Dominique could have sworn that his eyes were flooding with tears. He braced himself and remained there, immobile. He was dead. That he was not dead was impossible, but he did not fall back all at once—only with a slow sagging of his muscles.

His mother, overhead, had guessed nothing. She was busy showing the servant a page in her magazine. Who knows? A recipe?

The Cailles crossed the living room. They would shut the door with a slam, as usual. One day they would pull it off its hinges. The whole place shook with it.

On the other side of the street, an utterly calm Antoinette raised her head slowly, gave her brown hair a little shake, and moved a step forward. At that moment Dominique noticed a semicircle of sweat under Antoinette's arm, and she smelled her own all the more: both women's clothes were clinging to their skin.

The woman seemed not to look at the bed, as though she knew, as though she needed no confirmation. She did notice the white vial on the night table, picked it up, and looked around with sudden uneasiness.

The mantelpiece, opposite the bed, was chocolate-colored marble. In the middle was a bronze figure, a recumbent woman leaning on one elbow, and on each side was a pot holding a green plant with fine-toothed leaves, plants that Dominique had not seen anywhere else.

There was a step over Antoinette's head. The maid was about to come downstairs again. The medicine was uncorked. The drops were slow in falling. Antoinette shook the bottle, and the liquid fell on the greenish earth in one of the pots and was at once soaked up.

It was all over. Dominique would have liked to sit down, but she wanted to see everything. She was dumbfounded by the simplicity of what had occurred, by the natural way in which the woman on the other side of the street poured a last drop of medicine into the glass, another drop of water, and then went toward the door.

She could be felt, almost heard, calling:

"Cécile! Cécile!"

No one. She started walking. She disappeared. When she came back, the servant was with her. She had found a handkerchief on the way, and was biting at it, wiping her eyes with it.

"Go up and tell my mother-in-law."

Was it possible that her legs were not trembling like Dominique's? While Cécile rushed upstairs, she stood away from the bed, looking elsewhere. Her eyes wandered through the window, and seemed to be caught for an instant by the shutters behind which Dominique was watching.

Had their eyes met? It was impossible to be sure. It was a question that was often to torment Dominique. Her head was swimming. She would gladly have seen nothing more, gladly have closed the shutters tight, but she could not. The thought suddenly struck her that, a few minutes before, she had been gazing at her naked breasts in the mirror, and she was ashamed, she was seized with remorse. It seemed to her that that action, at that moment, was more shameful. The thought came, too—God knows why—that Antoinette was ten years younger, that she was not even thirty. Yet Dominique, who would soon be forty, often felt herself to be a little girl.

Never had she been able to convince herself that she was a grown-up, as her father and mother had been when she was little, and here was a much younger woman in action before her eyes. Here, while her mother-in-law, walking with the help of Cécile and another maid, was approaching, Antoinette was behaving with disarming simplicity, crying, wiping her eyes, explaining, pointing to the glass, asserting no doubt that the attack had been stronger than usual, that the drug had not worked.

The sky above remained the same threatening color of overheated slate; people came and went on the sidewalk like ants in the narrow trench their column had cut in the dust; engines turned over; buses panted; thousands, tens of thousands of people were frolicking in the blue water at the seaside; thousands of women were embroidering or knitting under yellow-and-red-striped umbrellas pitched on the warm sand.

Someone was telephoning, opposite. Monsieur Rouet, the father, was not there. He never was there. It was as though he had a horror of his home, where he was to be seen only at mealtimes. He went out and came back with the punctuality of a man obliged to get to his office on time, and yet it was years since he had sold his business.

Certainly Dr. Libaud was not at home. Dominique knew. She had sometimes telephoned him for her father at the same hour.

The women were at a loss. They seemed to be afraid, faced with this man, for all that he was quite dead; and Dominique was scarcely surprised to see Cécile come through the front door, go into the dairy, and emerge with Monsieur Audebal, who, in his white apron, followed her indoors.

Dominique was at the end of her tether. Her head was swimming. It was a long time since she had had her scanty midday meal, and yet her stomach was in revolt and she felt she was going to be sick. Still she hesitated to cross the living room, for fear of meeting one of the Cailles half-naked. Finally she remembered that they had gone out.

— 2 —

It had been about six o'clock the previous evening when Dominique had gone to mail the letter, a long way off, in the Grenelle district. Now it was not quite five o'clock in the morning, and she was up. How long had she slept? Barely three hours. She was not sleepy, she did not feel tired. For years she had scarcely slept at all. This had begun when she was looking after her father, who used to wake her every half hour.

Sometimes, alone in the one room she really lived in, she would move her lips, would almost pronounce words:

"One day, I must make someone understand. . . ."

No! She would write it. Not in a letter; she did not write to anybody now. She would record her many thoughts in an exercise book, and there would be a big surprise for whoever found it after her death. Among others, this: People who do not sleep, or who sleep little, are beings apart, much more so than people imagine, for they live every event at least twice over.

Twice! As she thought of this figure, she gave her

silent, suppressed little laugh, the laugh of one who lives alone. She had lived this event ten, fifty, a hundred times perhaps.

Yet she was not upset. Old Augustine could observe her from her attic, if she wished. She could see the everyday Dominique, with a kerchief tied around her head, a dressing gown of faded blue tied around her skinny waist.

It would not be long. In ten minutes at the most, Augustine's windows would be opening. She had nothing to do at five in the morning, but she did not sleep either.

All the shutters were closed; the street was empty and, seen from above, appeared so polished by the flood that had broken earlier that it was gleaming with violet reflections. Down where Boulevard Haussmann met Avenue de Friedland could be seen part of a tree. Although less than half of the greenery showed, the tree was truly majestic, despite the height of the surrounding buildings: living branches, a world of foliage of a somber green in which, all at once, a few seconds before the sun appeared in the sky, there would break out unsuspected life, a concert in which thousands of birds seemed to take part.

The window was wide open. Dominique never opened it until after she had made her bed. She felt ashamed of an unmade bed, of the crudity of crumpled bedclothes and dented pillow, even if they would be seen only by the one person who could catch a glimpse of them at that hour—old Augustine.

The gas was lit in the narrow kitchen that opened off the bedroom, and Dominique did her straightening and dusting mechanically, with the same movements she made every morning.

It was as if, at that time of day, her universe was extended. The whole street took part in it—the patch of pale blue sky above the roofs opposite, the tree at the Haussmann crossing. The bedroom seemed larger, like a room in the country opening straight onto a garden. Another half hour and the first bells of Saint-Philippe-du-Roule would be ringing. Occasionally a car would pass, and when one stopped two hundred yards away, Dominique knew that it was at the entrance of Beaujon Hospital—a sick or dying person being brought in, perhaps an accident case. She heard trains, too, far off toward Batignolles.

And her father, over the bed—her father in a general's full-dress uniform—was watching her. The portrait was so made that the eyes followed her into every corner of the room. It was company. It did not bother her, or make her sad. Had she not loved her father?

From the age of fifteen she had lived with no one but him, going with him to each of his garrisons. During his years of sickness, in this apartment on Faubourg Saint-Honoré, she had looked after him day and night like a nurse, like a Sister of Charity, and yet they had never been close.

"I am the daughter of General Salès . . ."

Involuntarily, she would pronounce his name in a special way, like a name apart, a precious, glamorous name. People did not always know "Salès," but "the General" was enough, especially when dealing with shopkeepers.

Do people suspect that the beginning of the day is

as full of mystery as the twilight, that it holds in suspension the same fragment of eternity? Dominique thought. You do not burst out into vulgar laughter in the fresh coolness of dawn, any more than at the moment when you are brushed by the first breath of night. You are more solemn, bearing the intangible pain of a creature confronted by the universe, because the street is no longer the commonplace, reassuring street, but simply a part of the great whole containing the orbits of the stars and the great body that touches the sharp angles of the roofs with gold.

They were asleep next door. Up close to the brown door, in which the key was on her side, she could catch the confused sound of their breathing; they were gorging themselves with sleep, just as they had gorged themselves with life all day long. The noises of the street would not wake them, in spite of their wide-open window; the clatter of the buses and taxis would blend naturally into their dreams, would sharpen their pleasure by giving them knowledge of their blessed state; and later, much later, at ten o'clock perhaps, slight noises, the movement of an arm, the squeaking of a spring, would be the prelude to the daily explosion of their vitality.

Strange that she had begun to feel a need of them! Still more since the drama, still more since the letter.

It had been about six o'clock when she set out to look for a distant post office, the hour of crowded café terraces, of glasses of beer on the little tables. There had even been men in shirtsleeves, their collars unbuttoned, as in the country.

She had gone on foot because she had to contain her

excitement by movement. She had walked quickly, with a somewhat jerky stride, and several times had run into other pedestrians.

She wondered now how she had been able to go through with it. Perhaps it was largely because of the power of words?

For three days the shutters opposite had not opened, for three days she had been living face to face with those masked features, as it were.

She knew, for she had been to see. She had not been able to stand it any longer. Besides, anybody had the right to go in. She had waited until the last minute, the previous afternoon at four o'clock precisely, after the men from Borniol's had come to nail down the coffin and had gone away again.

She had put on her black dress. The concierge had given her an indifferent glance from the depths of her lodge, and she must have recognized Dominique as someone from the neighborhood. On the third floor the apartment door was ajar; there was a silver salver in the brightly lit entrance. A man in black whom she did not know was sorting the visiting cards collected on it.

Was she, as she grew old, going to become like her Aunt Elise?

She took pleasure in breathing the odor, a pleasure that was almost sensual, and yet it was an odor of death, of candles, of too many flowers in closed rooms, with a musty hint of tears.

She did not see Antoinette. There was whispering behind a door to the left, that to the large living room. The bedroom door was open, and this room had been transformed beyond recognition into a mortuary chapel ablaze with candles. Five or six people were creeping silently around the coffin, to shake hands with old Madame Rouet, who was seated near a potted palm.

The gentlemen in heavy black suits and too-white linen were no doubt relatives from the provinces. They must be relatives on the Rouet side, like the girl scarcely out of school who was looking after the old lady.

Dominique had perhaps made a mistake. . . . No. She was sure she had not. In old Madame Rouet's attitude, in all her massive bulk, there was something hard and menacing. She was no longer the same person. It was impossible to laugh at her and her huge legs, her rubber-tipped cane and her air of ruling everything.

She had not allowed herself to be crushed under the weight of grief. On the contrary. She had grown still larger, more statuesque, as though her internalized sorrow supplied her with extra strength, even as it nourished her hatred.

Her hatred for the whole world perhaps, for everything that was not her son, including these nephews, who were here like groomsmen at a wedding and who in her eyes committed a crime by being alive. In any case, her hatred for the young woman who was somewhere behind a door and no longer had anything in common with the family.

Dominique had felt the shock of that maternal look and had been upset. It was as though the woman were capable of guessing her secret. Indeed, Madame Rouet looked at everyone coldly, sternly, seeming to say:

"Where does this woman come from? And that man, what does he want?"

She remained there, massive, rooted in her armchair,

without telling the rosary that had been put into her hand, without moving her lips.

Almost shamefaced, Dominique left the lying-in-state. In the hall she bumped against a woman from a well-known boutique, who was taking away a cardboard box. There was whispering behind a door; a fitting was going on.

Dominique had not been able to see Antoinette. She knew nothing of her doings, except that she had spent the last two nights in the apartment of her parents-in-law. Dominique had caught sight of the hem of her dress when she was shutting a window up there.

She had, on the other hand, caught a glimpse of the two slender-leafed green plants on the mantelpiece, which was draped, like the rest of the room, in black.

But for this glimpse, which lasted a quarter of a second, who knows whether she would have written? At home, she hunted high and low for an old work on botany, illustrated with copperplates, which she had long ago noted among the General's books.

The Cailles were out. She had once seen them eating in a cheap restaurant down the street, not far from the Madeleine, as cheerful in the midst of the crowd as in the solitude of their bedroom.

Kentia Belmoreana . . . Cocos Wedelliana . . .

The book smelled of old paper, the pages were yellowed, the print was very small, but at last she found the picture she was looking for. She was certain that the two plants across the street were *Phoenix Robelini.*

She took a sheet of paper from the drawer and wrote out those two words once, five times, ten times. After that she took another sheet and used them again as she printed:

27

The Phoenix Robelini on the right.

Nothing else. Was it not terrible enough? So terrible that she felt perspiration spring out under her arms and lose itself in the material of her underclothes.

The printed message made her feel ashamed when she was about to write the address on the envelope. It was shabby, almost ignoble. It smelled of the anonymous letter. She made do with sloping her handwriting backward, for she had read somewhere that all back-sloped handwriting looked alike.

Madame Antoinette Rouet
187 bis, rue du Faubourg Saint-Honoré,
Paris (VIIIe)

Now, alone in her bedroom, she no longer understood how she could have done it. She had had time for reflection. She had hurried far away, crossed the Seine, traversed the whole of the Ecole Militaire district. There was a holiday feeling in the streets. Numerous taxis on the way to the Gare Montparnasse were carrying beach gear or fishing tackle. She saw a canoe on the roof of a passing car. Those who remained in Paris must be thinking: Since everybody's going away, we're fully entitled to take it easy!

In the orange light there was a strange blend of calm and effervescence, a sort of truce with serious cares and daily preoccupations. Dominique had walked down unknown sidewalks, discovering provincial areas, where families sat on their doorsteps and half-naked children played in the street. She'd stopped finally, stopped short and sharp in front of a post office, where she got rid of her letter, and then stood there for another minute or two, trembling at what she had done, yet, in a way, relieved.

It was as though the Cailles had done it on purpose that evening. For seven years, since her father's death, she had lived alone in the apartment, and never once had she been frightened, never once had she conceived that you could be frightened of solitude. She had rejected the offer of a cousin who lived at Hyères, the widow of a naval officer, who had suggested she come to live with her there.

When Dominique had sent the advertisement of her room to the newspaper . . . how shameful to read, in print:

Furnished room to let to single person in handsome apartment on Rue du Faubourg Saint-Honoré. Low rent.

It had seemed to her that from that time her fall was public, definite. Yet it had to be done. There was no other way out. General Salès had no fortune. The sole property of the family had been a share—one-third—in this building, in which the General had settled after his retirement.

Did Dominique blame him? Hardly. She could look at his portrait without anger, as without pity. For a great part of her life, he had been for her merely a hairy man, always booted and with jingling spurs, a hard drinker who, when he entered the house, announced his presence with noisy shouts.

As a civilian, he had been nothing more than a querulous, mean old man, who seemed to blame passersby for not suspecting that they were rubbing shoulders with a general.

He had begun to gamble on the stock market. Then, after losing all he possessed, he had gone to bed, having selfishly decided to be an invalid, and leaving to Dominique the care of looking after everything.

Their share in the building had been sold. That Dominique still occupied her apartment was due to a cousin, now sole owner of the building, who allowed her the enjoyment of it. She had written to him, in her pointed hand, which gave the words a cruel look:

. . . I know how much I am indebted to you already, but in my present situation I am driven to ask you to agree to my taking a tenant. . . .

It was Caille who had come, because he was not well off and because, for the rent she was asking, he could have got only a tiny, bleak room in a hotel.

"You will have to go through the living room, but you will not meet me there often. All visitors are absolutely forbidden. You understand what I mean. Nor do I want any cooking done in the room . . ."

She had given him to understand that a maid would see to the housework, but the second day he had caught her at it herself.

"I haven't found anybody yet; I hope that in a few days' time . . ."

That was all the same to him. She had not dared say anything to him when she had found a Camembert box and a small piece of bread behind the overmantel. He was poor. He would sometimes eat in his room, though she looked there in vain for a gas ring. So he was not doing any cooking. He used to go out early in those days. He would come home late. He had two shirts and a single pair of shoes. She had read the letters he received from his fiancée and did not bother to hide.

It had been a whole epoch for her. She could not have defined it, but it left behind it regrets, nostalgia.

"I will never allow a woman in the apartment. . . . A man, all right . . . But a woman . . ." She had accepted Lina out of fear of having to advertise again, of seeing a stranger in her home.

"On one condition . . . Your wife will do the room herself."

Dominique was the one who regretted that now. She no longer had an excuse for going into the room at any hour. She did so still, but furtively, after having bolted the door to the landing. He still had only two shirts, but in the wardrobe hung the dinner jacket he had bought secondhand for his wedding. Lina left the most intimate things lying around in full view.

In the evening Dominique soon got into the habit of not going to bed until the couple had come in. What could they be up to so late? Long after theaters and cinemas had closed. They must wander around the streets, or into the little bars that were still open, for they had no friends. She would recognize their footsteps in the street a long way off. In their own room, they would go on talking loudly. They didn't hurry. After all, they could get up when they pleased. The sound of their voices behind the door grew into a kind of company Dominique could not do without. Indeed, when they were out more than usually late, she would lean on the windowsill to watch for them.

They might not shut the door properly. . . .

That was just an excuse. She did not want to take an interest in them. But that had not stopped her, the night before, from remaining at the window until two in the morning, watching the lights go out one after another and counting the passersby, while all the time she had under her eyes the closed shutters of the Rouets' apartment, which she knew to be the empty setting of the coffin in which the man with the colorless mustache had been finally enclosed.

She had reached the point of counting the hours that stood between her and the moment when he would be borne out at last, when the shutters would open and the rooms would come to life again.

The Cailles had come in. They talked! They were capable of talking like that from morning till night! What could they find to say to each other? She never talked to anybody; at the most, she sometimes caught herself silently moving her lips.

The letter would arrive this morning, at quarter past eight, carried by the little postman who walked crookedly, as though pulled over by the weight of his bag. The concierge would put it in the Rouets' pigeonhole, with the many letters of sympathy, for they had sent out a large number of announcements.

Dominique had one. She had stolen it. The Rouets, who did not know she so much as existed, had not sent one to her. The evening before, she'd gone into the lodge of her building, to make sure there was no mail for her. She scarcely got two letters a month now, but already an idea had come to her. She had at once seen, in the pigeonhole belonging to Madame Ricolleau, the wife of the former minister, who lived on the second floor, a large envelope with a black border.

She had taken it. The announcement was there on her worn tablecloth.

Madame Antoinette Rouet, née Lepron, Monsieur and Madame Rouet-Babarit, Monsieur and Madame Babarit-Basteau . . .

There was a lengthy column of them.

. . . regret to announce the death of their husband, son, grandson, uncle, cousin, nephew, second cousin, which occurred suddenly today after a long illness. . . .

Dominique's lips had drawn back as though affected by a nervous tic.

Now the street was beginning to liven up; other noises were mingling with the song of the birds in the tree. It was no longer possible to hear the fountain that ran night and day in the courtyard of the old mansion nearby. A truck pulled up to the curb opposite, and some men began work after rousing the concierge, who was in a bad temper. They were the undertaker's men, come to hang draperies surmounted by a silver *R* around the front door.

Old Augustine, who could see nothing from her window because of the cornice, soon appeared on the sidewalk, though it was much too early for her shopping. At Audebal's the milk was only just being delivered, and Sionneau's grocery was not open yet.

That day turned out like those which children enjoy too long in anticipation, so much so that they cannot sleep the night before, for thinking the day will never come.

Right up to the last minute the time passed with maddening slowness, and it seemed to Dominique that things were not taking place as they ought to.

For example, the undertaker's men, having put up their hangings, went off for a drink at the wine merchant's three doors down; soon they came out wiping their mouths and simply drove off.

As for the building's tenants, they left for work at

their usual hour as if nothing had happened. They passed between the draperies, and only a few turned around to judge the effect. The garbage cans took their places on the sidewalk. The shutters on the older Rouets' floor did not open until eight o'clock. But since these windows were higher than Dominique's, she saw the occupants only when they happened to be very close to them.

At nine o'clock two taxis stopped some minutes apart: relatives, some of those Dominique had seen the evening before at the lying-in-state. Every fifteen minutes or so, flowers were delivered by young girls or unimpressed boys. Quantities of flowers, although most of the friends of the family were on vacation. They must have telegraphed the florist.

Audebal's display had been set out as usual. Bégaud's pharmacy was open, and it too was framed in black and silver, like an undertaker's.

Dominique, already dressed, with her black thread gloves waiting on the table, was the only one to be ready too soon. The Cailles, after stirring on their bed for a moment, had gone back to sleep without even knowing there was a funeral across the street.

There'll be a lot of people, Dominique thought.

Various cousins were coming furtively to leave their cards, the ones who had no time to attend the ceremony or who assumed that their presence would be unwanted.

At quarter of ten, Dominique saw the manager of the boutique getting out of a taxi. She was bringing the dress!

The body was to be moved at half past ten! Antoinette, upstairs, must be waiting in her slip. . . .

Suddenly the street was crowded, though it was impossible to tell how. There were groups stationed on the

34

sidewalks. Ten, fifteen taxis arrived nose to tail, so people had to wait for the one in front to leave before they could get out in their turn.

A hearse turned up at last. An agitated movement seized all the black silhouettes, and when Dominique, judging that the moment for going downstairs had come, arrived in the street, the coffin was making its appearance in the vestibule, veils could be half seen in the semi-darkness, and bareheaded men were being directed to their places by the master of ceremonies.

No one suspected that the slight feminine silhouette nervously worming its way to the front was that of a woman who would give almost anything to catch the eye of the widow. Dominique knocked against one and another, stammered "Sorry," raised herself on tiptoe. She saw nothing but black garments, a veil, a rather common-looking woman in deep mourning supporting her daughter: Antoinette's mother had come.

Old Madame Rouet, on the other hand, did not appear.

Her husband walked behind his daughter-in-law at the same pace as when he set off each morning God knows where. He looked—the only one of the family to do so—at the people one after another, as though counting them.

What had taken so long to prepare happened too quickly. Dominique found herself surrounded by other women, took her place in a queue, mounted the steps of Saint-Philippe-du-Roule without seeing anything, and took her place in the north transept, a long way from Antoinette, whom she could see only from behind.

Perhaps she had not yet opened the letter, lost among so many letters of sympathy? Unconsciously, with a sort of voluptuous pleasure, Dominique took in the sound of the organ and breathed the scent of the incense, which brought back her childhood and those first morning masses during her years of religious enthusiasm.

As a girl, as a child, had she not got up before the others to go to mass, and had she not known that smell of the streets at daybreak?

If Antoinette were to turn around . . . Soon, when the procession was again in the forecourt of the church, she would pass very close to Dominique, would almost brush past her, and perhaps Dominique would get a view of her eyes through her veil.

There was something childish in this curiosity, something rather shameful. Early in her life, when there was talk in front of her about a girl who had had relations with a man, Dominique had afterward sought her eyes, as though she were going to find exceptional signs there.

One day, when they were living in Poitiers, her father's orderly had been convicted of theft. And Dominique had observed him in the same fashion. When she was smaller still, she had walked around and around a lieutenant who had gone up in an airplane.

Such things in life made a strong impression on her—Lina, her tenant, too. Often she would spend hours wrestling with herself, because of that door which separated them, that keyhole through which she could look.

Tomorrow, I will do it. . . .

Then she used to forbid herself. She was sickened by the thought of what she would see. Afterward she felt really ill, as though the inmost secrets of her own flesh had been violated. But the temptation was not to be resisted.

And Antoinette Rouet—she had been so hungry for life she'd stood unmoving while her husband died. She had let the seconds run out one by one, without stirring, without a movement, her hand on the doorjamb, knowing well that each of those seconds was a second of agony for the man in the bed she herself had slept in.

Afterward she had not so much as looked at him. She had thought of the medicine. Her gaze had strayed around the room, had settled on one of the green plants.

Phœnix Robelini.

The plant had remained in the death chamber. It was still there among the draperies that the undertaker's men must be busy taking down. She would see it when she got home. Would she dare do away with it?

Would she go on living in the Rouets' building? Would they keep with them, close to them, a daughter-in-law who was no longer anything to them and whom old Madame Rouet detested?

At this thought, Dominique was panic-stricken. Her hand clenched on the pew in front of her. She was afraid she might be robbed of Antoinette, and all she felt now was the need to get back to Faubourg Saint-Honoré, to reassure herself that the shutters were open as usual and that life would go on in that apartment.

Had it not been a bad omen seeing Antoinette at her mother's side, as if she were already changing families once more? Why had she not been at the lying-in-state the evening before?

Because old Madame Rouet did not wish it!

Dominique was sure of that. She did not know what had happened, or what would happen, but the previous evening she had seen the old lady, as massive and hard as a caryatid, and she had sensed that a new feeling had entered her being. . . .

Some relatives, distant relatives in the furthest reaches of the family, turned around to inspect the congregation, and the liturgy rolled out its monotonous splendors. Dominique mechanically followed the comings and goings of the officiating priests; her lips from time to time accompanied their prayers with a murmur.

She filed up for the offertory. Old Monsieur Rouet, bolt upright, looked at the faithful as they passed one by one, but Antoinette had knelt down and was keeping her face between her hands.

She was behaving like an ordinary widow, a black-edged handkerchief crumpled into a ball in her hand; and when at last she passed close by Dominique, the latter, seeing only eyes a little more brilliant than usual and very smooth pale skin—perhaps because of the lighting and the veil—was disappointed. Then immediately afterward something struck her. She wondered for a moment what it was. Then her nostrils quivered, and in the air, heavy with incense, she identified the delicate scent Antoinette Rouet trailed in her wake.

Had she really used perfume?

When Dominique stepped out into the forecourt, amid the monotonous crunching of soles, she encountered a dazzling triangle of sunlight. The first cars were moving off, to make way for those behind, and she slipped into the crowd and away, to avoid the burial, hastening her pace the nearer she got to home, on the shady Faubourg Saint-Honoré.

The Rouets' shutters were open. The Cailles had only just got up, and the water was running into the tub in the bathroom. The phonograph was playing, and a faint smell of gas and breakfast coffee was still in the air. Dominique, on opening her window, welcomed with relief the sight of the windows opposite, out of which Cécile and another maid, plying duster and broom, were driving columns of luminous dust.

— 3 —

It was violence that burst out, where Dominique, her impatience turning to exasperation, had expected to see fear or perhaps remorse. And that violence ran white-hot, like a force of nature, so freely that for a while Dominique could not understand what was going on.

It was the fifth day after the funeral, and nothing had happened yet. The weather was much the same, the sun as fierce, with this difference: now, toward three o'clock the sky would become leaden, the air heavier, and unhealthy emanations bore right down on the Audebals' dog lying across the sidewalk. People's eyes turned automatically upward in hope, the hope of seeing this lowering sky break up at last, but, though indistinct rumblings sometimes seemed to be audible, far away, the storm did not break, or moved off to break far away from Paris.

Her nerves taut, Dominique had done nothing during these five days but wait; and she could now no longer have told which would relieve her more—the unloosing of the elements or the event for which she was watching for hours at a time, which she could not foresee, yet which could not fail to happen.

It was inconceivable that across the street Antoinette should be living as though suspended, as though in an overnight hotel, as though in a railway station. By way of convincing herself, Dominique would whisper over and over again:

"She hasn't read the note. Or else she hasn't understood it. Perhaps she doesn't know the name of the green plant."

Antoinette was once more sleeping in the big double bed, the one that had been her husband's sickbed, the one in which he had died. She went out very little. When she did, she wore her mourning, but at home she had not given up the luxurious négligées she was so fond of; they were richly trimmed heavy silks.

She would get up late, after idly eating breakfast in bed, and exchange a few words with Cécile. It was clear that the two women did not get on with one another, Cécile appeared stiff and reserved, and Antoinette bore her presence with obvious impatience.

She would wander around the apartment, tidying drawers, making piles of the dead man's clothes, calling the maid to carry them off to some distant closet.

She would read. She read a great deal, something she never did before, and it was rare to see her without a cigarette in a long ivory holder. What a lot of time she was able to spend seated on a divan polishing her nails or in front of a little mirror solemnly plucking her eyebrows!

Not so much as a glance at the windows opposite.

She ignored Dominique, she ignored the street, coming and going as though she attached no importance to it in this provisional universe.

It was not until the fifth day, around nine o'clock in the morning, that the suitcase incident occurred—or, rather, the two suitcase incidents, for, by an odd coincidence, a suitcase played a part in Dominique's apartment too.

Dominique had, shortly before, gone out to do her shopping. There had been a trivial incident. At Audebal's three or four women were standing in a group by the white marble counter. The proprietress had served her first, not as a favor, but because some regular customers were in the habit of stopping for a moment to gossip while unimportant shoppers were swiftly disposed of.

"What can I do for you, madame?"

"Two ounces of Roquefort."

Dominique's voice was flat and sharp. She was not going to be ashamed of admitting her poverty, and she deliberately looked the gossiping women straight in the eye.

Madame Audebal weighed the cheese. The women were silent.

"There's just a little over. . . . One franc fifty . . ."

It was too much. She could afford only one franc's worth of cheese. Her expenditures were meticulously calculated, and she had the courage to say:

"Would you kindly weigh me exactly two ounces."

Nobody said a word. Nobody laughed. Nevertheless, there passed through the clean white shop a current of ferocious pleasure as the proprietress carefully set about dissecting a tiny morsel of Roquefort from an already small piece.

When she passed under the archway of her building, Dominique was surprised to see Albert Caille, who had come downstairs in his pajamas to find that there was no mail for him. He seemed surprised and put out, and determinedly rummaged through all the tenants' pigeonholes.

She went upstairs and peeled a few vegetables. A little later she heard lengthy whispering in the Cailles' room. Lina got up, and dealt with her dressing much more quickly than usual. The couple was ready in less than ten minutes, and it was then that the first suitcase was introduced.

Dominique recognized the sound of two metallic clicks. Frightened by the thought that her tenants were going to leave her, she stood close to the living-room door. She half opened it and soon saw them going out. Albert Caille was carrying his suitcase.

She did not dare stop them or question them, but contented herself with shooting the bolt behind them. She went into their untidy bedroom, then to the bathroom, where she saw their toothbrushes, his unwiped razor, some washing hanging up to dry. She saw the dinner jacket in the wardrobe. Then, because old Augustine was at her window up there, she felt embarrassed and went back to her own room.

Why had they taken the suitcase away? Last evening they had not gone out for dinner as usual, and yet she had not seen them come in with little packages, as people do when they want to eat something at home.

Old Madame Rouet was at her post—in her tower,

Dominique used to think—that is, seated by the window over the room where her son had died. It was a window that went up from the floor, like all the windows in the building, so she could be seen from head to foot, always in the same armchair, her cane within reach. From time to time she would ring for one of the maids, give orders to some invisible person, or, facing the dim interior of the room, would supervise some job she'd given instructions for.

Several minutes elapsed before Dominique saw Antoinette, who must have been in the bathroom. Then suddenly she was there, in a pale green dressing gown, her hair slightly out of order, helping Cécile drag a rather heavy trunk into the middle of the room.

Dominique's heart thumped.

She's going away. . . .

So that was why she'd remained so calm! She had been waiting for the formalities to be over. The day before, a somber-looking man, who must be the family lawyer, had come. Monsieur Rouet had not gone out as usual. Antoinette had gone upstairs to her parents-in-law, no doubt for a sort of family council, for a settlement of affairs.

Now she was going away, and Dominique's impatience was becoming exasperation, then rage. A thousand thoughts assailed her and yet she could not have said why she was refusing to allow the departure of Antoinette Rouet, why she was determined to oppose it by every means.

She'd even thought of going to see her! But no. She had only to write:

I forbid you to leave. If you do, I will tell all.

Undergarments and clothing piled up in the trunk.

The two women went to another room for suitcases and cardboard boxes.

Antoinette was cool. Cécile was more rigid, more disapproving than ever. While her mistress was arranging some jewels in a little casket, she disappeared.

Dominique guessed what that meant, and was pleased with herself for having guessed right. She had only to look up. The time to climb one flight of stairs, to knock. Madame Rouet turned her head and said:

"Come in!"

She listened, frowned, raised herself from her armchair, using her cane for support.

Dominique was triumphant. And she looked at Antoinette with a sardonic grin—as much as to say:

"Oh, so you think you're going to get away as easily as that. . . ."

She was expecting what happened; yet the actual sight was so striking that it gave her a shock.

She saw Antoinette quickly turn her head. At the same time she saw old Madame Rouet framed in the doorway. She had come downstairs and was standing there, massive and unmoving, leaning on her cane. The old lady did not speak. She just looked. Her gaze moved from trunk to suitcase, to the unmade bed, to her daughter-in-law's green dressing gown, to the jewel casket.

It was Antoinette who was disconcerted. It was she who, jumping up like a schoolgirl caught breaking the rules, launched into a flood of speech. But even as she began, one cutting word silenced her.

What had she been trying to explain? That she had no reason for staying on in Paris in mid-August, in such heat? That the family had always spent the summer in the country or by the sea? That her mourning would be

45

no less mourning somewhere else than in a dreary and stuffy apartment?

But what she was faced with, what her hunger for space and movement beat against, was a cold, unchangeable force. It was centuries of tradition, a reality on which the realities of life could gain no hold.

At one moment the tip of the cane was raised. It touched the skirt of the green silk dressing gown, and the gesture sufficed. It was more than a condemnation; it was an expression of utter contempt, contempt the old lady's features would not condescend to register, leaving the task to her cane.

Old Madame Rouet disappeared. Left alone, Antoinette looked at herself in the mirror for a long time, her fists clenched against her temples. Suddenly she strode to the door and called:

"Cécile! . . . Cécile!"

The maid emerged from the invisible rear of the apartment. Words flowed and flowed, while Cécile, as impassive as her old mistress upstairs, stood rigidly, refraining from lowering her eyes.

She was a scrawny girl, very dark-skinned, with no style, who wore her hair scraped to the back of her head, where it formed a hard bun. Her complexion was sallow, her chest flat. While she listened patiently, she kept her hands folded across her stomach. Those folded hands proclaimed her self-confidence as well as her contempt for all the anger that broke around her but did not touch her.

Dominique could not hear the words. Without realizing it, she moved so close to the window that if Antoinette had turned her way, she would have known that she had long been under observation, and would perhaps have learned much more at the same time.

Her brown hair, loose and abundant, floated around her head, and its silken mass swung from one shoulder to the other. Her dressing gown was partly open, her half-naked arms gesticulating. Her eyes moved incessantly back to those hands folded in effrontery across a stomach.

Finally, Antoinette could stand it no longer. In a real explosion, she hurled herself on Cécile. She hurled herself on those hands and tore them roughly apart. When the maid still did not budge, she gripped her by the shoulders, shook her, banged her head several times against the door.

Just then Cécile looked out the window for a second or two, unconsciously, no doubt, or perhaps because a puff of air lifted a fold of the curtain. Her eyes met Dominique's, and Dominique was sure she had caught the shadow of a smile.

Of a terribly satisfied smile!

You see! Now you know what she's really like, this woman who made her way into our house, who pretended she was living with Monsieur Hubert and who now . . .

That suppressed smile, was it not really directed at Antoinette?

Hit away! Throw yourself around! Show yourself for the slut you are! Look more and more like what you really are, a fishwife off the streets, like your mother, who sold shellfish in the market . . . You're being watched! You don't know it, but you're being watched and you're being judged. . . .

Antoinette let go. She took three or four steps across the room, still talking passionately. When she turned around, she was dumbfounded at finding the maid still in the same place, and she threw herself on her again, with more force. She pushed her into the boudoir next door, hustling her along, almost pulling her off her feet, until she reached the door to the landing.

She threw her out. Perhaps she locked the door. And when she appeared again, she was almost calm. The outburst had relieved her, but she was talking to herself, walking up and down, wondering what to do, since she still had an overmastering need to act.

Was it the sight of the unmade bed, with the breakfast tray on the coverlet?

She went to the telephone and dialed.

In her tower, old Madame Rouet had turned toward the interior of the room. Cécile was there; no doubt of it. The old lady was not getting up again. She was listening. She was speaking calmly.

At the telephone, Antoinette was being emphatic. Yes, it must be at once. Dominique did not know what Antoinette had decided on, but she understood that it had to happen *immediately*.

There were moments when Dominique forgot to breathe, so much did this energy throw her off balance. She had been less impressed by the crime itself—and it was undoubtedly a crime that had been committed under her eyes. At least that had taken place silently, without movement. It had been merely the climax of a secret, suffocated life, whereas now life overflowed, turbulent and encroaching, with its fearful rawness.

Dominique didn't know what to do with herself. She didn't want to sit down. She didn't want to miss anything

48

of what was taking place, yet it hurt her, made her giddy. It was even more painful than when she had looked through the keyhole—like the first time, for instance, that she had seen the sexual act in all its brutality, and had witnessed the thrust of a man's body quivering with animal strength.

So this was Antoinette? Dominique's whole being was revolted by this splendid, vulgar craving for life.

She wanted to write, at once. The words that kept coming to her were as crude as the spectacle she was witnessing.

You killed your husband.

Yes, that was what she would write, immediately. And that was what she wrote, without thinking, without taking care this time to disguise her handwriting.

Instinctively she added:

You know you did!

And those words betrayed Dominique's inmost torment, the true reason for her indignation. She could have understood remorse. She could have understood anguish slowly distilled by the hours as they passed. She could have understood everything, made allowances for everything, pardoned everything perhaps, except this lack of feeling, this five-day wait and subsequent brisk departure—for if Antoinette had not been stopped, she would have left, naturally and cheerfully! Most important, she could not pardon the rebellion, which revealed Antoinette's lack of awareness.

"You know you did!"

No doubt; but Antoinette did not seem to realize the fact. She might know it, but she did not feel it. She was a widow. She was at last freed from a dull and boring husband. She was rich.

She was leaving, and why not?

Dominique nearly went downstairs at once to mail her letter, but a truck drew up across the street, and two men got out, laden with tools, two workmen in blue coveralls.

Antoinette received them at the front door of the apartment. Cécile had not reappeared.

She was calm. Her movements were precise. She had made up her mind. She knew what she wanted, and her decision would be carried out forthwith.

The first thing to do was to dismantle the huge bourgeois bed and remove it. The upholsterer's men took off the mattress and placed it near the doorway. Then they unscrewed the bedposts. At once the room appeared naked, with nothing but a square of fine dust to mark the place where Hubert Rouet had died.

Antoinette kept giving orders, bustling around without a thought for her half-open dressing gown, and followed by the two men, who obeyed, unconcerned, carrying into the bedroom the divan on which she had slept while her husband was ill.

She glanced at the somber curtains, which were hardly ever drawn, and nearly said:

"Take them away!"

No doubt the thought struck her that the windows could not be left uncurtained, and that there were no other curtains at hand.

The two pots, with their green plants, were still on the mantelpiece, and one gesture settled their fate. Dominique could not believe her eyes when she saw Antoinette let them go without a look or a tremor, without a thought of all that had happened.

The Cailles were still out. It was eleven o'clock, and the street was almost deserted. The pharmacist had lowered his faded yellow awning, and the closed shutters of some shops suggested a Sunday morning.

As early as half past eleven the upholsterer's men had finished their work, had moved the furniture around and had stacked the superfluous pieces in a room overlooking the courtyard, the dim light from which Dominique glimpsed for one instant at the end of a long perspective of doors.

Then, left alone and contemplating her surroundings, Antoinette seemed to say, with a certain satisfaction:

"Since they want me to stay! . . ."

She was reorganizing herself, emptying the trunk and the suitcases, lighting a cigarette from time to time, shrugging her shoulders after a glance at the ceiling, above which she could feel the overwhelming presence of her mother-in-law.

Did she suspect that events were going to rush to a climax and make that day a turning point? In any event, she was at her ease in activity, welcoming it with relief. She did not bother to dress or go out to lunch; Dominique saw her come out of the kitchen with a piece of cold meat on a slice of bread.

Old Monsieur Rouet came home. Dominique saw him only in the street. His wife disappeared from the window, and it was easy to imagine the two of them in the half-darkness of their apartment. She was giving him the news, and they were considering steps to be taken.

Indeed, a little later Antoinette jumped when she heard her door bell ring. By the second ring, she was on her way to open the door. Her father-in-law entered, cold and calm—less cold, however, than his wife, as if he had come to soften sharp corners.

He must have been instructed, up above:

"Be firm! Above all, be firm! Don't let yourself be worked on by her tears and her pretenses. . . ."

Perhaps to give a more serious tone to his visit to the apartment that had formerly been almost common to the two households, he had brought his hat; and, as he sat, he balanced it on his knee, shifting it each time he crossed or uncrossed his legs.

"My dear, I have come . . ."

That was how he must be speaking.

". . . after the painful time we have just lived through . . . obviously you must understand that . . . obviously it is necessary . . . if it were not for other people . . ."

It was a fresh source of stupefaction for Dominique to see Antoinette perfectly calm, almost smiling, an Antoinette who said yes to everything, though with more irony perhaps than conviction.

Of course she would do without a vacation, since her parents-in-law made such a point of it! She had merely taken the liberty of making the apartment more habitable for a single person. Was that a crime? Was she not entitled to arrange to her liking the place where she was condemned to live? Well, that was all. Perhaps after a while she would change the curtains. They were far too mournful for a young woman. She had said nothing before because it was her husband's taste, or, rather, the taste of her parents-in-law. . . .

Even Monsieur Rouet must be delighted to find her so amenable. But he still had one demand to put before her. He hesitated, shifting his hat two or three times, biting off the end of a cigar, which he did not light.

"You know that Cécile is one of the family, so to speak, that she has been with us for fifteen years . . ."

A man is rarely able to perceive hate in a woman, because it does not show itself in the same way as with him. He never notices the slight raising of the bosom, the scarcely visible start, the slight transient tensing of features, then the condescending smile.

Well! It was agreed: Cécile could come back. . . . She would continue to spy on Antoinette, to go upstairs ten times a day to her mother-in-law's for orders and to tell her everything that took place downstairs.

And then? . . . Anything else?

Come, come! No excuses! Quite natural! Just a little misunderstanding. Everyone's on edge in this stormy weather. . . .

She escorted her father-in-law to the door. He wrung her hand, delighted that the interview had passed so well, and hurried up the stairs, two at a time, to tell his wife that he had been victorious all along the line, that he had displayed firmness and inflexibility.

And look! There was Cécile already, going downstairs again, faultless in her black frock and white apron, her voice as sharp as her features:

"What would madame wish me to bring her?"

Ah! She had eaten, thank you. She did not need anything. Just a telephone call, because the emptiness, after all these comings and goings, was less endurable today, like the drafts on a spring-cleaning day.

It was a telephone call full of familiarity and affection. That was obvious from her face and the way she smiled.

She was talking to someone she trusted, because the smile momentarily was full of menace toward a third party.

"That's agreed, then. Come . . ."

While waiting, she stretched out on the divan, her eyes on the ceiling, her long cigarette holder between her lips.

The Cailles had still not come in.

Dominique's letter was on the table, close to the little package in which the Roquefort had become soft and sticky.

Would she send it or not?

She was not a shellfish seller. It was true that her father had been a fish salesman in Dieppe, but she—Antoinette's mother—had married a man who worked for the Métro. So she had never lived behind a fishmonger's slab, still less in the market.

She was tall and stout, and her voice must be deeper than the average woman's. She had taken care to trim her half-mourning with a white band around the brim of her hat. The way she paid off the taxi, after inspecting the meter, was enough to reveal a person with no need of a man to guide her through life.

She was not alone. A young woman, not more than twenty-two, was with her. She was not in mourning, and she had not been present at the funeral. There was no need to look twice at her to realize that she was Antoinette's younger sister.

She was wearing a very smart outfit and a hat by a celebrated house. She was beautiful. That was the first thing that struck you. Much more beautiful than Antoinette, with something more reserved about her that disturbed Dominique, something, moreover, that Dominique did not understand. She could not say whether this was a girl or a woman. The large eyes were a dusky blue and very calm; her manner was more reserved than her sister's. Her upper lip had an upward curve, and that perhaps was what contributed most to her air of youth and candor.

Antoinette had not needed to dress for them. They kissed, and with a look Antoinette announced:

"The old lady's up above!"

She let herself fall into an easy chair, motioning to her sister to take the divan. But her sister contented herself with a chair, maintaining the attitude of a young lady paying a call.

She was perhaps too trim and correct, which made one think of a woman after all.

"Tell . . ."

That was what her mother must be saying, as she examined the walls and the furniture around her. The way Antoinette shrugged her shoulders was commoner than when she was by herself. She was speaking. It was clear that her voice was commoner too, with a slight drawl, and that she must be using words that were not particularly well-bred—especially when she referred to the old lady in the tower and her eyes automatically sought the ceiling.

During the whole of Antoinette's married life, Dominique had never seen the sister enter the apartment, and she could easily have counted the times she had seen the mother. It was easy to understand why.

Since their arrival the apartment had changed; the atmosphere was now one of carelessness and disorder.

Antoinette's mother had dumped her hat on the bed. Soon perhaps, overwhelmed by the heat, she would stretch out on it, while the sister alone maintained the attitude of a refined caller.

Antoinette was still telling her story—miming her mother-in-law's arrival, her apparition, rather, framed in the doorway, the comings and goings of her creature Cécile. She mimed the wheedlings of her father-in-law, his false dignity. She made fun of it all, trying to force a laugh, and her final gesture seemed to conclude:

"So much the worse for them!"

It was quite unimportant, mind you. She would manage. She *was* managing. She had plenty of time. Come what might, she would get her own way in the end, in the teeth of all the Rouets in creation.

Had old Madame Rouet, up above, heard the sound of raised voices? Anyway, she rang, and began to question Cécile as soon as she came to see what was wanted.

"It's madame's relatives, her mother and her sister . . ."

No! Not that! The mother . . . all right, but the sister! The sister, who . . .

"Please ask madame to come up and see me."

Antoinette was hardly surprised at the request.

"What was I telling you? Wait a second . . ."

Was she going to go upstairs in her dressing gown, in the too-green dressing gown at which the cane had so recently pointed such angry scorn? What good would that do?

She took down a black dress, the first that came to hand, and planted herself in front of the mirror. There she stood in her slip, before her mother and sister, ar-

ranging her hair, sticking in hairpins she took from between her teeth.

"Does that look all right?"

Better get going! She climbed the stairs. Though
Dominique could not see her, it was as if she was following her with her eyes. Madame Rouet's once beautiful
profile was eloquent. No rage. Just a few words, which
broke from her like ice from a window.

"I thought it was understood, once and for all, that
you would not have your sister here. . . ."

Down below, Antoinette's sister knew what was going
on. She was already on her feet, primping in front of
the mirror, waiting only for Antoinette's return to take
her leave.

It was done.

"And that's that! She laid down the law all right! All
I've got to do now is to show you the door, my poor girl.
The old cow says so."

She burst out laughing, and her laughter across the
street hurt Dominique. She kissed her mother, then
called her back, went to a little bureau, and took out
some money.

"Look! At least take this . . ."

Antoinette was asleep on the divan, one foot hanging
almost to the floor; and on her face there was no trace
of the least emotion or anxiety. With lips half parted,
she was sleeping in the afternoon heat, with all the life
of the street humming around her.

The Cailles had not come in, and Dominique had
once again visited their room, after bolting the front
door.

57

She knew now that they had not gone away. In the wardrobe she had failed to find Lina's coat, a fine winter coat of beige cloth trimmed with marten, which she had brought with her from home—a brand-new coat such as a well-off bourgeoise from the provinces would own.

Dominique had gone out and, right up to the last minute, had put off making a decision. Yet, very furtively, she had dropped her letter in a box on Rue Royale. A bus crowded with foreigners had brushed close by her, and it seemed to her that these transient visitors, dazzled by the strange city, were escaping from the common stream of life.

Her breast had been pinched with envy. She had never had any money or time to spare, over and above the monotonous and disheartening daily round—apart from a few short years, long ago, before her eighteenth birthday: but she had not realized it then, and so had not been able to relish it.

Only that morning she had had to insist that fat Madame Audebal, her bête noire, pare off a scrap of cheese because the piece already cut was too big and too expensive. Everything was too expensive for her!

The Cailles had gone out to sell Lina's coat, or perhaps they had pawned it: but they lived as though they had no need to count their money.

They lived! Just then she saw them, walking arm-in-arm. She sensed that the suitcase knocking against the man's side was empty. She sensed especially, from his greedy lips and the sparkle in his eyes, that he was rich, that he had money in his pocket, that now he was going to live even more grandly. And Lina followed him without a thought of where he was leading her.

Dominique would have preferred to slip by unnoticed, but Lina had seen her and had pinched her companion's arm as she murmured something. What was it?

"The landlady . . ."

Yes, that was what she was to them! Unless Lina had said:

"The old hag!"

Did she think one felt old at forty?

And here was Caille greeting her with a great bow —bowing to one, so humble and slight, who hugged the wall as if to take up less room in the street.

And these thousands of people hurrying to and fro, slumped happily on café terraces, drinking, talking, looking at women's legs and their too thin frocks clinging to their rumps—all this smell of human bodies, of human life, seized her by the throat, mounted to her head.

How terribly, terribly she longed, that day, to burst into tears!

— *4* —

She walked quickly, as if she were being followed. And the nearer she got to home, the more precipitate and jerky her gait became. Her feverish activity was like that of a swimmer who suddenly realizes how rash he has been and swims frantically toward shore, to be within his depth again.

That was exactly it. She was beginning to get back to her depth at the entrance, where she was welcomed by the hollow echo peculiar to this former house converted into apartments. Her feet met once more the rough grain of the loose yellowish flagstones. She saw her reflection, tiny and misshapen, in the brass knob at the bottom of the stairs, and her hand slid with physical contentment along the polished railing. Higher up, invariably on the same step, she paused a moment to hunt in her bag for her key; each time she did this she suffered a little pang, because she never found the key at once, and, half-seriously, she would wonder whether she'd lost it.

She was home at last. Not yet fully at home in the living room, but only in the bedroom, the one room to which she had confined herself and which she would sometimes wish smaller still, the better to charge it with herself.

She locked her door and stood, tired and out of breath, at the spot where she always stopped, in front of the mirror, seeking in it her own reflection by way of welcome.

She looked for herself, for Dominique, once called Nique—but who, except herself, would have called her that now? She felt for Nique an overwhelming pity, and it did her good to look at her in this mirror that had followed the Salès family to all the garrison towns from the time she was a child.

No, she was not yet an old maid. Her face remained unwrinkled. Her skin remained fresh, although she lived cooped up indoors. She had never had much color, but the skin she saw was of a rare fineness, and she would recall the voice of her mother saying, with such delicate inflections:

"Nique has the skin texture of the Le Brets. As for the way she carries her head, she gets that from her grandmother de Chaillou."

It was a comfort, on coming in from the rough tumult of the street, where people shamelessly displayed their vitality, to be back with her household gods, as it were, with certain names that were not mere names but the enduring landmarks of a world she formed part of and revered.

The syllables of those names had a hue, a scent, a mystic significance. Nearly every one of them was represented by some object in this room in which Dominique was now regaining her self-possession, with the taste of the street still in her mouth.

There was neither alarm nor clock in the room, but a tiny gold watch at the head of the bed. This watch, in its case decorated with a flower in pearls and ruby dust, was the watch of her grandmother de Chaillou. It evoked a vast country house in the neighborhood of Rennes that everybody used to call the chateau.

"The year the chateau had to be sold . . ."

Serving as a casket for the watch was a red silk slipper embroidered in green, blue, and yellow. It was Nique who had embroidered it, when she was seven or eight years old and was a boarder with the Sisters of the Ascension in Nîmes.

She lit the gas and laid a napkin at the end of the table by way of a cloth. They must be having dinner in most of the apartments on the street—those at least whose occupants were not away on vacation—but no one was to be seen in Antoinette Rouet's room.

To get away from this obsession with Antoinette, to whom her thoughts kept incessantly returning, Dominique wanted to play her game, to play at thinking, as she used to call it, and indeed still did, half wittingly, half unwittingly.

It needed a particular disposition of spirit. You must put yourself in a state of grace. In the morning, for instance, when she was occupied with the housework, it was impossible. It was impossible, too, to begin at a set moment. It was like a waking dream, and dreams do not come on order. At the most, you can only put yourself progressively in a favorable state.

The name *de Chaillou* was a good one to start from,

a key word, but there were others; for example, *Aunt Clémentine*. . . . Aunt Clémentine—that would be in the morning, around eleven o'clock, when the coolness was giving way to the more oppressive noonday sun and you began to be aware of the smell of your skin. . . .

A villa at La Seyne, near Toulon . . . Aunt Clémentine's husband—she was a Le Bret who had married a Chabiron—was an engineer at the arsenal in Toulon. . . . Dominique was spending a month's vacation with them; she was reading, in a garden blooming with mimosa. As the sun beat fiercely down, she could hear the panting of the engines at the naval dockyards. She had only to get up to see, through a tangle of gantries and traveling cranes, a patch of sea of an intense blue. And it was all so still, formed a whole so close-knit, that it was a relief at midday to hear the rending shriek of the factory sirens answered by the sirens of the ships at anchor and followed by the tramping feet of the workmen as they crossed the tracks.

Aunt Clémentine was still alive. Her husband had died long since. She was still living in her villa, alone with an old servant. And Dominique, in spirit, set each thing in its place, right down to the russet cat, which could no longer be alive; she reconstructed each corner. . . .

Suddenly, because she used to play this game while watching over her sick father, she began to tremble, thinking she heard the well-known sigh coming from the bed. She was disconcerted not to see the old General in his place, with his hairy face and that look which always expressed icy reproach.

"Well? Where's my pipe?"

He smoked in bed, he had given up shaving, and he

hardly ever washed his face. It was as though he was dirty on purpose, deliberately growing into a repulsive object, and he would sometimes say, with diabolic satisfaction:

"I'm beginning to stink! Admit that I stink. Go on! Admit it. It's true! I stink; my God, I do!"

Her father's room—now it was the Cailles'. She no longer needed to play at thinking, to look for subjects for her dreaming. Antoinette and the old Rouets were across the street, and near her, separated from her by a single door, were the young people now returning with their empty suitcase.

What were they doing? What was this bustle? She was not used to it. It was not their time of day. They had scarcely had time for dinner. Why were they not off to the cinema, or the theater, or one of those dance halls whose tunes she used to hear them humming next morning?

A bucket was being filled. The tap was wide open. They were quite capable of forgetting it and letting the water spread over the floor. She was always afraid, with them, of some such disaster, because they had no respect for things. For them, a thing, no matter what, was something that got replaced. It cost a certain amount, and that was all. Whereas she would fret over a spot on a mat or curtain! They were talking, but they were making too much noise moving things for her to be able to catch the words. Augustine was at her window. She had taken up her post. For her it was a real post of duty. Her supper was barely finished before she was leaning her elbows with all her weight on the attic windowsill. She had on a black blouse with a tiny white pattern, and the violet shadows of evening brought out the whiteness of her hair. There she was, placidly dominating the streets and roofs. It was not until much later that one window or another filled with people coming for a breath of fresh air now that their day was done.

Dominique had played the game with old Augustine, too, on days of depression, when the mirror returned an image full of fatigue, with black-ringed eyes and colorless lips—on days when she felt old.

What had old Augustine been like at the beginning? What had she been like at forty? What did she do then?

The story of Augustine invariably ended with her funeral, which Dominique would visualize down to the smallest detail.

"What is it?"

No. She had not spoken those words. It was inside her that the question had framed itself. There had been a knock on the door. And she looked around with anguish, wondering who could be knocking at her door. Such was her surprise that she had not thought of the Cailles. There was a pause long enough for someone to walk up and down once or twice, and then there was another knock. She turned the key soundlessly—she did not want it thought that she lived behind a locked door. Glancing in the mirror to make sure there was nothing untidy about her appearance, she put on a tense smile: one must smile when people call.

That was another relic of her mother, who had had a smile of infinite melancholy.

"It costs so little and it makes life so much pleasanter! If everybody would only make a little effort . . ."

It was Albert Caille. He appeared embarrassed. He, too, was doing his best to smile.

"I beg your pardon for disturbing you . . ."

She thought: He's come to tell me they're leaving. . . .

And he, despite his good upbringing, peered into the mysterious recesses of this room in which she lived. What was it that astonished him? That she confined herself to a single room when there were others she could use? That it contained nothing but ill-assorted and old-fashioned furniture and objects?

"We have had a letter from my parents-in-law. They arrive from Fontenay-le-Comte at eleven o'clock tomorrow morning. . . ."

She was surprised to see him blush, he who was always so much at ease in life. She noticed that his features were assuming a childish expression, that of a child who wants something, who is afraid he will be refused, and pleads with a pout.

He was so young! Never had she seen him so young! He still had some innocence left beneath all his smart ways.

"I don't know how to explain. . . . That we're not yet settled in our own apartment is because my job may change from one day to the next. . . . You understand. . . . My parents-in-law are used to their comfortable provincial life. . . . It's their first visit to us since our marriage. . . ."

She had not thought to ask him to come in. She did so now, but he remained near the door. She guessed that Lina was waiting, listening.

"I'm so anxious that their first impressions be favorable. They will only be here a day or two: my father-in-law can't leave his business for long. . . . If, during that time, you could let us use the living room as though it were ours . . . I'm quite prepared to . . . provide a supplement to the rent. . . ."

She was grateful to him for having hesitated and then not pronounced such a coarse word as *pay*.

"We'll be out all day, in any case. My parents-in-law will be staying in a hotel."

He thought she was hesitating, but she was thinking:

Does he take me for an old maid? Do I look so old to him? Am I in his eyes a woman, a woman like . . . a woman to whom . . .

She saw again the spectacle she had several times watched through the keyhole, and she was troubled, ashamed of herself. Not for anything in the world would she permit a man, whoever he might be . . . But to know that a man, that Caille, for instance, might have such an idea . . .

"My wife would also like . . ."

He said "my wife," which meant that still-unfinished creature, with her shape not yet set, that bran-stuffed doll, so to speak, who laughed at everything and because of everything, showing teeth that might have been milk teeth.

"My wife would also like, just for these two days, to make one or two little changes in the room. . . . Don't be alarmed. We'll put everything back. We'll be very careful."

Would he venture, for example, to come close to her, to put out his hands as he surely did with other women, for he had the innate urge to explore anything that was woman's flesh?

He smiled. His look was suppliant, disarming.

"What do you want to alter in the room?" she heard herself saying.

67

"If . . . if it would not trouble you too much, I would remove the head and foot of the bed. Oh, I'm used to that sort of thing. With just the mattress we'd have a divan, and we have got a cover for it. . . . You understand?"

Wasn't it extraordinary? That morning, Antoinette Rouet had done exactly the same thing across the street! Thus, in her and in the young couple was an identical taste, and Dominique thought she understood. They no longer thought of the bed as a means of rest; they were making something else of it, something more sensual, adapting it to other ends and activities.

"You will let us? Do say you will."

She realized that her blouse was again wet under the arms, and the feeling of damp warmth made her eyes sting. Very quickly, she said:

"Yes. Go ahead."

Then, on second thought, she added: "But mind you don't damage anything!"

They would laugh at her, because of that warning. They would say:

"The old girl's afraid for her furniture and her old-fashioned curtains."

"Thank you very much. My wife will be so glad."

He withdrew. In the living room Dominique saw flowers—a whole armful of fragrant flowers had been laid on the marble top of a table until they could be arranged in various vases.

"Oh, don't put any in the blue vase. It's cracked, and the water would leak . . ."

He smiled. He was satisfied. He was in a hurry to be close to Lina.

"Don't worry . . ."

68

All that evening they led a noisy life. There was the sound of buckets being filled, of washing and scrubbing and furniture being polished. Twice Dominique saw Albert Caille busy doing housework in his shirtsleeves.

She had shut the door tight to get some slight feeling of being in her own home. She leaned out the window, lightly, nonchalantly, as though just for a moment, and not with the static force of old Augustine, who was clearly determined to remain at her post for hours. The street was quiet and almost empty. A very thin old man, dressed all in black, was exercising a small dog and stopping patiently each time the dog stopped. The Audebals were sitting in front of their shop door. It was obvious that they had been on the go all day long, that they had been hot, and that they had only a few minutes to relax, because the husband had to be at the market at four in the morning. Their helper, the one who carried the milk and whose hair was always falling into her eyes, was sitting by them, her arms dangling, her eyes empty. She was probably not more than fifteen, yet she had the big breasts of a grown woman, like Lina, perhaps larger. Who knows if she had not already . . .

Of course! With her boss! Audebal was the sort of man who made a most unpleasant impression on Dominique. He was so sturdy, so full of hot blood, that one seemed to feel it beating in his arteries with great strokes, and his eyes had the arrogance of a high-spirited animal.

Occasionally, from Boulevard Haussmann, voices could be heard. It was a group walking along and talking loudly, as though for the benefit of the entire universe, regardless of the people leaning from their windows or taking a little turn in the coolness.

The light was brassy, and there were brassy glints on

the houses. A brick chimney looked as though it were bleeding. On the shadowed side of the street colors assumed a terrifying depth. The least animate objects seemed to be alive. It was as if, with the day finished and the turmoil hushed, at this hour when men were putting a damper on their existence, things were beginning to breathe and to live their own mysterious lives.

The windows of Antoinette's bedroom had just been shut. Dominique had caught a glimpse of Cécile's black dress and white apron. For one second she had seen the bed in all its intimacy, its cover already turned down. Then the curtains were drawn; they filtered a faint pink glow, the glow from a lamp with a pink shade, which had been placed on a table a few minutes before.

Was Antoinette, like a prisoner, going to bed already? Right over her head, old Madame Rouet was at her post, with her husband beside her. Of him Dominique could see only a patent-leather slipper, a patterned sock, and the bottom of his trousers. He had one foot on the support bar of the window.

They were talking without heat or hurry. At one moment the old lady would speak; Dominique saw her lips moving. The next she would fall silent and turn toward the interior of the room to listen to what her husband had to say.

Dominique was impatient for it all to be over, for the people to disappear one after another—first the Audebals, dragging the legs of their chairs over the sidewalk and letting loose a metallic din as they fixed the iron bars on their shutters; then the pale woman she did not know who lived to the left, on the third floor of Sutton's leather-goods shop. Dominique had often met her with a child of five or six: it was very well cared for, and its mother felt impelled to stoop over it constantly. But the child must be ill, because it had not been seen out of doors for at least a fortnight, and the doctor went into the house every morning.

Yes, let it all disappear! She would even prefer to see the shutters hermetically closed, as in winter, because at this time of year there were people who slept with their windows wide open, so that it seemed possible to feel the breath of the sleeping beings exhaling from the windows. The illusion was so strong that, for an instant, it seemed to Dominique that some sleeper had just turned over on his damp bed.

The birds in the tree—that portion of tree she could glimpse at the end of the street, where a policeman patrolled, not knowing what to do with his white truncheon—the birds had begun to show the same ecstasy as in the morning, an ecstasy that would come to a sudden stop when the last reddish gleams had died away and the sky, now an icy green in the quarter opposite the sunset, had gradually taken on the softness of night.

She was not sleepy. She seldom was. The Cailles' spring cleaning irritated her, upsetting her world. She jumped at every noise, worrying and wondering what they were doing to her home. She wondered, too, why Antoinette had gone to bed so early. How could she go to bed and sleep peacefully after the day she had just gone through, in the room where only a few days earlier her husband, bathed in mortal sweat, had appealed desperately for help, with his whole being, with as much voice as a fish thrown down on the grass and gulping greedily at the death-dealing air.

The hours, the half-hours, sounded from Saint-

Philippe-du-Roule. All the light of the day had melted away, but shafts of light soon appeared along the ridges of the roofs opposite—rays of a moon soon to emerge from behind those roofs and reminding Dominique of the great square at Nancy when she was little and the first arc lamps shed the same frosty rays, so sharp that they pierced your pupils.

There was no one left to go in now except fat Augustine. Soon she shut her window. She would be slumping down on the bed with all her weight. And, heavens! what sort of nightclothes would she be in? She could be visualized enveloped in shapeless things, camisoles, drawers, and flannelette petticoats charged with her own special smell.

Dominique had not put on the light. Under the door a strip of light came from the Cailles' quarters. They had left their window open; it was possible to make out the lighter rectangle projected on the darkness of the street.

It was one o'clock when they put their light out. The pink light had gone out across the way, too, at Antoinette's. On the floor above, the Rouets were in bed.

Dominique was alone. She gazed at the moon. Quite round and of an unearthly fullness, it had finally climbed a few inches above a chimney. Because the sky was too pale, forming a single luminous surface, like a ground-glass window, the stars could scarcely be distinguished, and some words came back to Dominique's memory:

. . . *killed by a bullet in the heart, at night, in the open desert* . . .

Only a sky like this could give the idea of the desert. An equal solitude underfoot and overhead, and this moon sailing in a limitless universe.

. . . at the head of a column of twenty riflemen . . .

She turned around. On the sewing-machine cover, she could make out, despite the darkness, the shape of a prayer book, its binding protected by a black cloth cover. It was the missal that had been given to her for her first communion. One of the cards, on fine illuminated parchment, bore her name, with the initials in letters of gold.

Another pious picture in the missal was on a mourning card.

Madame Geneviève Améraud, née Auger, died, fortified by the rites of Holy Church, in her . . .

Angoulême. Her father was only a colonel then. They were living in a huge square house, a very soft yellow in color, with a wrought-iron balcony and almond-green shutters for the windows, which opened on a boulevard with a track for riding. The garrison bugles were heard punctually at five o'clock in the morning.

Madame Améraud was a widow who lived in the house next door. She was tiny and used to walk with very small steps, and a saying was:

"As gentle as Madame Améraud . . ."

She smiled at everybody, but more readily at Nique when she was fifteen or sixteen years old. She used to invite her into the living room, where she would spend hours of monotony without seeming to guess that the girl's continual haunting of her house was on account of her son, Jacques.

Yet he was to be seen only during vacations, for he was a cadet at Saint-Cyr. He wore his hair *en brosse*. He had a serious face and a serious voice too. It was astonishing, this bass voice in so young a man, who had as

73

yet only soft down on his face. But the seriousness was gentle.

"Nique . . ."

For three years exactly she had loved him, all to herself, without telling a soul—loved him with all her heart, living only in the thought of him.

Did he know? Did Madame Améraud know the reason for the young girl's being daily in her house?

One evening the colonel had been invited to call. Old brandy had been served, liqueurs and cinnamon biscuits. Jacques was wearing the uniform of a second lieutenant, and he was to leave the next day for Africa.

The lampshade was pink, like the one in Antoinette's bedroom. The window was open on the boulevard, where they could see the moon reflected from the pale trunks of the plane trees that glowed with its light. They heard the last bugle call sound at the barracks.

Dominique had been the last to go. Madame Améraud had discreetly withdrawn; the colonel was waiting on the sidewalk while he lit a cigar; and then, in a whirl, during the brief moment Jacques held her hand in his, Dominique had stammered out:

"I'll wait for you always . . . always . . ."

A sob mounted, she withdrew her hand, and, to get away, took her father's arm.

That was all. Except for a postcard, the only one she had received from him, giving a view of a little baked-mud post on the edge of the desert, the black silhouette of a sentry, the moon, and, near that pallid moon, one word, followed by an exclamation mark:

"Ours!"

The same moon as had shone on them that evening in Angoulême, and the same moon Jacques Améraud was to be killed under *"by a bullet in the heart"* in the desert.

Dominique leaned forward a little through the window, so that her forehead could catch the cool breeze whispering past, but then she recoiled with a blush. From the next window sounds reached her—a murmuring she knew well. So they were not asleep! Their room arranged, the flowers in the vases, the light out, it was *that*, still *that*, which claimed them; and the most shocking thing, perhaps, was the abrupt laughter, stifled but all the more eloquent, of a woman being made happy.

Dominique longed to go to bed. She withdrew to the back of her room to undress, and, though there was no light on, her body showed white in the shadows. She covered herself hastily, and made sure that the door was shut. As she slipped into her bed, she gave a last look at the window opposite and saw Antoinette leaning on the sill.

No doubt she had been unable to get to sleep. She had turned on the pink lamp again. Its light revealed the disorder of the divan converted into a bed for the night, the pillow on which a hollow showed the mold of her head, the embroidered sheets, an open book, a cigarette smoldering in its holder.

The room seemed to be pervaded by a voluptuous atmosphere of softness, and Dominique hid behind one wing of the window in order to observe Antoinette outlined in the sharp clarity of the moonlight. Her brown hair, let loose, flowed over milk-white shoulders. Her body, in a heavily embroidered silk nightgown, had a ripeness that had never before been revealed to Dominique. One word sprang to her lips, one simple word, *woman*, and Dominique thought she understood it for the first time. Her arms resting on the wrought-iron bar, Antoinette was leaning forward, so that her bosom spread slightly over the whiteness of her arms; her breasts were gently pushed up; a shadowy hollow could be seen in the opening of her nightgown. Her chin was rounded, and it, too, rested, as it were, on a little roll of softest flesh.

A short time ago, when the two sisters were face to face, Dominique had judged Antoinette's sister to be the more beautiful.

Now, she understood. It was a being in full bloom that was there in the setting of the cool of the night, on the frontier between a pink-lit room and the infinite.

It was a being in suspense, as it were, a being which had been made for something, which was yearning after that something with every fiber. Dominique was sure of this. She was quite taken aback by the pathetic look of the dark eyes staring at the sky. She could feel a sigh which, swelling breast and throat, was exhaled through full lips before the teeth, in a sort of impatient spasm, could close on it.

The certainty came to her that she had been wrong, that she had behaved like a fool—not like a child even, but like a fool, like the foolish old maid she was. And she was overcome with shame.

Shame for the letter whose naïve riddle was like the riddles schoolchildren amuse themselves with:

The Phoenix Robelini on the right.

And, confronted with Antoinette's tranquillity during the days following the dispatch of the letter, she had been lost in conjecture, thinking that Antoinette had not received the note, that perhaps she did not recognize the name of the green plant!

What did it matter to Antoinette?

Dominique had thought, only a short time before, to deliver a decisive blow. Yes, there had been malice in her action! Or, rather, a dumb instinct for justice—envy, perhaps?—what did it matter? Only a short time before, like an old maid in a frenzy of excitement, she had scribbled another note, thinking to be cruel, to plow furrows in the flesh with the point of her pen:

You know quite well that you killed him!

Was that what she had written? No!

You killed your husband. You know you did.

Did she know? It mattered so little! Nothing mattered except that living flesh which had fled from the pink-lit divan and was now, for all its immobility, its quiet appearance of a woman at her window, nothing but an irresistible urge toward the life it needed so much.

Dominique, standing barefoot, hiding like a criminal behind the wing of the window, blushed for herself— for having understood nothing, for having seen only the most obvious and sordid details of what had taken place opposite, for having feasted on them, even today, as she spied on the entrance of a menacing mother-in-law, the diplomatic attitude of an embarrassed father-in-law, Antoinette's glad relapse into vulgarity when with people of her own kind, the money she had furtively taken from a drawer and handed to her mother—everything, even the pink light, the nightgown in too heavy silk, the cigarette smoldering away in the long ivory holder.

So fixed was her attention on another's life that she forgot to breathe herself. Her burning gaze stayed riveted on the woman at her window, on those eyes lost in the sky. From them she drew a more vibrant life, a forbidden life. She felt the blood beating in her veins, a fit of giddiness taking possession of her, and suddenly she threw herself down on her bed, burying her face in the softness of the pillow to stifle the bitter cry of impotence tearing at her breast.

For a long time she remained thus, rigid, her teeth clenched on the linen now wet from her saliva, haunted by the feeling of a presence.

She is there. . . .

She did not dare make a movement. She did not dare turn over. She waited vigilantly for the slightest noise that would put an end to her torment, that would bring the news of her delivery. It came, a long time later, long after the Cailles, flesh against flesh, had gone to sleep. It was the commonplace squeaking of a window catch.

At last she could raise her head and turn half over. There was nothing left except a closed window, the dull opacity of the curtain linings, a passing taxi—and only then did she allow herself to sink into sleep.

— 5 —

What use would it be to invoke her familiar ghosts? They would only gather around her like saints you're not sure of, in whom you already have ceased to believe, yet from whom you furtively seek pardon.

The air was liquid. Her things were in their places, with their colors, their solidity, their play of light, their comforting humbleness. They were within reach of her hand, because Dominique's aim had been to reduce her universe to the four walls of a room. Yet at that hour it was as if she also owned the visible world beyond the pale blue rectangle of the window, the great space of morning freshness in which the smallest sounds made an echo, for even old Augustine was not yet up.

Dominique was pale. Her features were drawn. Neither cold water nor soap had been able to dispel the traces of the bad hours she had passed in the camp bed—the bed that now, at quarter past five, when the first steps echoed in the street, had already resumed its severe counterpane and its innocuous appearance of being something made ready for parade.

For years, indeed throughout her life, Dominique had made her bed as soon as she rose, in a hurry—she did not quite know why—to clear her surroundings of everything that could recall the life of the night. It was only this morning—she had awakened with a dull pain in her head, an abnormal sensitivity of the temples—only this morning that this obsession had struck her. Her eyes had sought another ritual object, the wicker basket that contained the stockings waiting to be darned and the big egg of varnished wood.

Instantly a softer, almost sweet atmosphere had lapped around her. She had felt the presence of her mother. With an effort she could perhaps have seen her face, elongated like those of the Virgin in pious pictures, the smile that radiated from her without being expressed by any particular feature, her hand that, as soon as the doorbell rang, reached for the stocking basket in order to hide it in a cupboard.

"You don't let people see your stockings in holes."

No more did you let them see those shapeless things, all too evocative in their intimacy—stockings rolled into a ball. Never, during the day, would a half-open door have permitted a glimpse of the foot of a bed or the marble, livid as a nude, of a washbasin.

Search her memory as she might, Dominique could not recall her mother in a négligée, or in her slip, or even with her hair unbrushed.

One phrase kept coming back to her now, and she realized, at forty, that the influence of this phrase, seemingly so simple, had pervaded her entire life. Where had it been spoken? Dominique found it somewhat difficult to place herself once more in the various houses they had occupied, because she had lived in the same atmosphere everywhere. The Salès' houses resembled one another as do hotels of a certain class. They were big light houses—oddly enough, almost every one had had a balcony—with trees close at hand, on a square or a boulevard, in localities inhabited by doctors and lawyers, and, nearby, always the sounds of a garrison.

An uncle they did not very often see had called. There was a little gathering in the living room. Dominique was perhaps fourteen years old. She had not yet been sent to bed. The talk had turned to dogs and their instinct.

"It's solely by smell that they recognize people. I know a blind old lady who begins to sniff whenever anybody passes by, and immediately afterward she gives the name. Never makes a mistake . . ."

Madame Salès had given that constrained smile, made that imperceptible movement of the head, which was automatic with her when upset. Had she already guessed that Dominique would be asking her:

"Is it true, Mama, that people have a smell?"

"No, dear. Uncle Charles doesn't know what he's talking about. It's only people who don't wash who smell."

What use would such a mother's gentle and melancholy shade be to Dominique when she peeped at the closed windows behind which Antoinette Rouet was drugging herself with sleep?

All Dominique's ghosts were of the same kind, as were all the sayings she found in the depths of her memory.

"The Cottrons have gone to take a cure at La Bourboule. . . ."

You did not specify the name of the disease; you did not evoke the ailing flesh.

"Little Madame Ralet has just had a baby. . . ."

The expression "given birth to" did not come in to sharpen the picture. Everything always occurred in a world of halftones, whose inhabitants never appeared otherwise than washed, brushed, and smiling or sad.

Even the proper names were like fetishes. They were not uttered like ordinary words, like the names of people in the street. They had their peculiar noble quality. There were half a score of them, not more, with admittance into this vocabulary, which was the meeting place of the family at Brest, the family at Toulon, the lieutenant colonel and the naval engineer and the Babarits, who had made an alliance with the Lepreaus and thus entered the sacred circle by right of second-cousinage with the Le Brets.

Yet these people, it occurred to Dominique today, had not been rich. Most of them had only a little property.

"When Aurélie inherits from her aunt de Chaillou . . ."

The Rouets, with their millions, would never have been allowed access to the magic circle. Nothing rough or common was allowed to enter, nothing coarse, nothing smelling of everyday life.

Indeed, only ten days previously, Dominique had been watching the lives of the people opposite with a contemptuous curiosity. She had been interested in them because their windows were under her eyes from morning till night, in the same way as she was interested in old Augustine, and the woman with the sick little boy or even—though, God knows, a gulf separated them—the unspeakable Audebals.

They had been nothing to her; there was no mystery

about them. Common people who had made a fortune out of manufacturing wire—old Monsieur Rouet had founded one of the most important copper-wire works in the country—and who led such a life as they were fit to lead.

That an Antoinette should have entered their household—that was commonplace: a bachelor of forty, feeble in constitution and character, who let himself be seduced by a typist because she was a pretty girl and knew what she wanted.

That was the simple, harsh light in which Dominique had been observing them for years.

She has gone out again in the car. . . . *She* has got a new outfit. . . . *Her* new hat is extravagant. . . .

Or else:

He doesn't dare say anything to her. . . . *He* is over-awed by his wife. . . . *He* lets himself be led by the nose. . . . *He* is not happy. . . .

Sometimes she would see them in the evening, alone together in their room, and it was clear that they had no idea what to do or what to say to each other. Hubert Rouet would pick up a book, and Antoinette would pick one up in turn, but she would quickly throw it aside or gaze over the top of the pages.

"What's the matter?"

"Nothing."

"What would you like to do?"

Didn't he understand that she didn't want to do anything, that she couldn't do anything, *with him*?

"Are you bored?"

"No . . ."

Then, most often, she would rearrange her clothes closet and her odds and ends, or else she would lean her elbows on the window bar and gaze out like a prisoner, waiting for bedtime.

Yet, only ten days ago, Dominique would simply have summed the situation up, as her mother would have, with the gentle smile of those who are above such temptations:

"You can't be happy if you marry outside your own set."

The Rouets' set was quite uninteresting. The set Antoinette came from did not, so to speak, exist for them.

"No, dear. It's only people who don't wash who smell."

When, near nine o'clock, Cécile came to open the curtains and the window, and lay the breakfast tray on the bed in which Antoinette was leaning back against the pillow, Dominique's nostrils quivered, as if, from across the street, it was possible to catch the scent of the young woman stretching there in the sunlight, swelling with life, her eyes and her lips greedy, her flesh rested from the voluptuous pleasure of sleep.

Caille had left early for the station, where he was to meet his parents-in-law, and Lina was giving the last touches to her rooms. She could be heard humming as she moved between the bedroom and the living room, which was charged with the scent of the flowers.

The mailman had finished their block by quarter past eight. Antoinette would soon receive the letter. But Dominique no longer expected anything from that letter. She felt ashamed of it, and like someone who has struck out in blind rage with some harmless weapon and has not caused even a scratch.

It would not have taken much, so disgusted was she

with herself, to prevent her from watching. She was tempted to choose that moment to go and do her shopping. She felt empty. She was floundering, as you do in those vague dreams that come toward morning after a bad night. Her room seemed lamentably dreary, her life feebler than the little flame in front of the altar that always seems on the point of going out. The memory of Jacques Améraud was growing dim, and she felt a grudge against old and gentle Madame Améraud, as if *she* had encouraged her in her renunciation.

How many times since her mother's death had she not heard the women of the clan—Angibauds, Le Brets, de Chaillous—say to her, with uniform unction:

"Your mother, my child, was a saint!"

She had not tried to clarify these words. Any more than, as a little girl, she had been allowed to ask the meaning of the sixth commandment, to pronounce, otherwise than as an incantation, "Thou shalt not commit adultery."

What had happened, sometime in her sixth or seventh year, to transform the atmosphere of the house? Her memories were vague, yet vivid. Before that time there had been laughter, real laughter, around her. She had often heard her father whistling in the bathroom. They went out together on Sundays.

Then her mother had been ill and had stayed in her room for long weeks. Her father became serious and furtive, and seemed always to be kept away from home by his duties, or else he shut himself in his study.

Never had she heard the least allusion to what had occurred.

"Your mother was a saint. . . ."

85

And her father was a man! This characteristic came to her suddenly, with blinding clarity. Her father smelled of tobacco, of drink, of the barracks.

Her father, in short, from the time she was six or seven, had no longer been part of the family. It was no longer he—it was only Lieutenant Colonel Salès, later the General—who belonged to the clan. Not the man. Not the husband.

What terrible offense had he committed for him to be thus outlawed, for his wife to be no more than the shadow of a woman, a shadow growing fainter and fainter and finally flickering out altogether while still quite young? What had he done that she, Dominique, had never loved him, had never been tempted to love him, had never wondered why she did not love him?

She met her own gaze in the mirror, and she made an effort to soften its harshness. She knew that she was in the process of calling to account her ghosts, all those things—comforting shadows, bright memories, scents of bygone days, pious objects—that had borne her company in her solitude like muted music.

Across the street, Antoinette was yawning, running her fingers through her heavy tresses and stroking her bosom. Turning toward the door, she must be saying:

"What is it, Cécile?"

The mail. Before reading it, she sat on the edge of the bed, hunting for her slippers with her bare toes, and her calm shamelessness no longer shocked Dominique. She understood now, and she could have wished Antoinette more beautiful and more glamorous still, attended by a train of servants as she stepped into a marble bath.

Old Madame Rouet was in her tower. She was another who would never let herself be seen in négligée, who seemed to emerge from the night in full armor, her features already hard and her eyes cold and clear.

Antoinette was still yawning, then drinking a sip of coffee, tearing open an envelope, putting a bill down beside her on the bed, then another letter, of which she read only the opening lines.

Soon it was the turn of Dominique's message. Antoinette opened the envelope without looking at it, read the few words of the note, frowned as if she did not understand, and then, quite naturally and calmly, picked up the envelope from the bedside rug, where it had fallen in a crumpled ball.

You killed your husband. You know you did.

How Dominique would have liked to take it back from her! How utterly childish were the words that had sought to be vengeful and cruel, how foolishly harmless the weapon!

She had killed her husband? Perhaps . . . But no, not really. She had not prevented him from dying.

And her words were hateful by the sheer weight of their silliness:

You know you did.

No. Antoinette did not know it, she did not feel it. And the proof was the way she reread the letter in an effort to understand, remaining pensive for a moment, without once looking at the window opposite. She was thinking.

Who could have done this spiteful thing?

Not a glance, either, at the mantelpiece, where the green plant—to think that Dominique had looked up its correct name in a work on botany!—where the green plant had still been standing the day before!

To the contrary, when she raised her head, it was toward the ceiling that she turned, toward the tower where her jailer was on guard duty.

The old lady?

Why should she have written to her?

Antoinette shrugged her shoulders. That was not it. Was she going to wear herself out searching further? Was she going to worry and fret?

She let the sheet of paper fall by the others, and went to the window to breathe the air of the street, to fill her eyes with the splashes of sunlight and the moving figures. Doubtless she was still giving a little thought to the matter.

No! It was not her mother-in-law. She, true enough, was convinced that Antoinette had killed her son, but not in that way. It was a feeling, rather than a certainty or even a suspicion—the feeling a mother would naturally entertain toward the detested widow of her child.

Oddly, Dominique was suddenly afraid Antoinette's gaze would come to rest on her window, on her, on her skimpy shape scurrying around a room she was now ashamed of. She went to shut the window, taking care not to be seen.

The noise began on the stairs, a floor below—cheerful talk, a man's big voice, a woman's laugh—then Albert Caille, extremely animated, fumbling as he tried to find the keyhole, an overdone exclamation of wonder, the vulgarity of which made Dominique think of flushed wedding parties leaving suburban churches.

Lina rushed forward, exclaiming:

"Mama!"

She must be lingering in her mother's arms, because Papa's big voice grumbled humorously:

"Now then, don't I count any more?"

Dominique could see nothing and yet she called up a colorful scene—crude colors, big solid masses, a clean-shaven man, well dressed and smelling of eau de cologne, very proud of himself, an important provincial manufacturer, very proud of coming to Paris to see his married daughter for the first time.

Lina was playing the guessing game.

"What is it?"

"Guess."

"I don't know. . . . Give it to me."

"When you've guessed . . ."

"A dress?"

"Dresses aren't brought from Fontenay-la-Comte to a young lady living in Paris."

"The box is too big for jewelry. Give, Papa!"

"When you've guessed . . ."

She grew impatient, stamping her foot as she laughed, crying out to her mother:

"I forbid you to rummage in my chest of drawers. Albert! Stop Mama from upsetting our things. . . . Now, Papa, be good. . . . Ah! I knew you'd give in. Where are the scissors? Albert, hand me the scissors. . . . It's . . . What is it? . . . Wait! A divan cover! Come and see, Albert! . . . Just the shade of pink I adore. Thank you, Papa. Thank you, Mama."

Why did her mother begin speaking in a low voice? Because they were talking about the landlady, no doubt. Where is she? What is she doing? What is she like? Is she nice to you?

She was answered in whispers. Dominique could

have sworn that the father had taken off his jacket, and that the sleeves of his immaculate shirt made two dazzling splashes of white in the room.

These people were not members of the clan either. Their exuberance touched Dominique on the raw, in her inmost, her most Salès–Le Bret nerve fibers. Nevertheless, she could find certain points of contact, particularly in the whispering of the mother, whom she pictured as small and rather fat, dressed in black silk, with two or three pieces of jewelry, which she wore only on important occasions.

Quickly, she changed her clothes, putting on her best dress, glancing around to make sure there was nothing untidy about her. An automatic reflex made her look at the photograph of her father in a general's full-dress uniform, with his medals hanging on the frame.

Another rapid look, across the street, through the glass of the windows and the muslin of the curtains, a look in Antoinette's direction, to ask her pardon.

The whisperings were not in the bedroom now, but in the living room. There was a cough. There was a gentle knock on the door.

"Excuse me, madame. I am Lina's mother. . . ."

She was tiny and dressed in black silk, as Dominique had imagined her, only thinner and livelier—one of those women who spend their lives running up and down the stairs of a too big provincial house in pursuit of disorder.

"I hope I'm not disturbing you?"

"Not in the least, I assure you. Do, please, come in."

The words came of themselves from very far away, as did the slightly reserved attitude and the overdone smile, with, however, a suitable touch of melancholy, and

90

a touch, too, of the indulgence proper in the case of newlyweds.

"I wanted so much to thank you for all the kindness you are showing to these children. . . . I must ask you whether they disturb you too much. I know them so well, you see! At their age, one is not often thoughtful about others. . . ."

"I assure you I have no grounds for complaining of them."

The door had been left open. The living room was empty, and the flowers were in their places. Dominique would have taken a bet that Lina was eying her husband as she restrained her longing to burst into laughter. . . .

"Mama is with the dragon."

Perhaps they had held a whispered discussion before taking this step?

"You go alone, Mama. . . . I swear it's better if you go alone. I couldn't keep a straight face. . . ."

"Come with me, Jules."

"No. Look now, it's much better for women to get together about that sort of thing."

They had watched her go. They were all there listening. . . . In a few minutes the mother would be telling them that Dominique had put on her best dress to receive her.

"Won't you sit down . . ."

"I'll only stay a moment. I would hate to disturb you. . . . We would have preferred to see the children settled in their own place, with their own furniture by now. Especially seeing that my husband manufactures furniture . . . They didn't want to. They say they'd sooner get to know Paris well first and then choose what district

91

to live in. . . . My son-in-law has his career to think of. He's doing very well already, considering his age. . . . You've read his articles?"

Dominique, not daring to say yes, slowly nodded by way of affirmation.

"We are so glad, my husband and I, to think they are with someone like you. . . . Not for the world would I have had them stay in a hotel, or some boarding-house. . . ."

A glance at the portrait, the decorations.

"Your late father?"

The same slight affirmative gesture of the head, with that infinitesimal touch of prideful humility that sits properly on a general's daughter.

"I hope you won't take it amiss that my husband and I have taken the liberty of bringing you a little memento to show how grateful we are—oh, yes, grateful—for what you are doing for the children."

She fetched a package from the living-room table; she'd not dared make her entry with it in her hand. Dominique guessed that it had not been brought for her. There had been a whispered argument in the bedroom.

"Better give it to her. I'll send you another one. . . ."

It was a little alabaster bedside lamp, which they had taken from their shop, for they also went in for interior decorating.

"Nothing very special . . ."

She did not know what else to say. She had had time to glance around once or twice, so she'd seen everything. She smiled.

"Thank you once again. I won't take up any more of your time. . . . We are only staying in Paris until to-

morrow evening, and we still have everything to see.
. . . Good-bye for now, madam. If the children make too
much noise, or if they don't behave, don't hesitate to
speak to them about it. . . . They're so young!"

That was all. Dominique was alone. Silence next
door, where the mother had rejoined the family. More
on her guard than her daughter, she had spotted the
communicating door and she must have put a finger to
her lips. Lina held back the laugh she would have liked
to let out. A moment or two, while they found their
normal voices, and then the mother spoke deliberately
loudly:

"Suppose we take advantage of its not being too hot
yet, and go to the zoo at Vincennes?"

The spell was broken. They all talked at once and
got ready in a hubbub. The noise made its way into the
living room, tailed off toward the double door and faded
away on the staircase.

Dominique was really alone. Automatically she took
off her dress and lit the gas, which made a plop. Since
the window was shut, she could not be seen, so she remained in her slip, as if in defiance.

Defiance of whom?

Was it of these people—their name was Plissoneau
—all dressed up to visit their daughter in Paris?

Yet another marriage which might not run smoothly.
The Plissoneaus were more than comfortably off. Albert
Caille was a policeman's son. From time to time he sold
an article or a story to a paper, but was that a career?
Why, the very way Madame Plissoneau had spoken of
it . . .

Why did she remain half-naked, intentionally, looking at herself each time she passed in front of the ward-

robe mirror? Was it Antoinette, who took no interest in her, and who probably did not even know of her existence—was it she that Dominique sought to defy?

Or was it her ghosts—which she never called up now without a bitter look, as though they had shabbily betrayed her?

Was it not really herself she was defying, as she let the raw daylight play on the pallid skin of her legs and thighs, her angular shoulders and her neck set between two salt cellars?

See what you are, Nique! See what you've become!

Nique! They had called her Nique! Her aunts and her women cousins still called her that in their letters. For they did write to one another from time to time— at the new year, or for a marriage, birth, or bereavement. They exchanged news of one another, using first names that evoked mere children and yet referred now to grown-ups.

"Henri has been posted to Casablanca and his wife complains of the climate. You remember little Camilla who had such lovely hair. She has just had her third baby. André is worried, because she is not strong and she won't look after herself properly. He's relying on Aunt Clémentine to make her understand that in her condition . . ."

Nique! Nique and her long crooked nose, which had caused her so much suffering!

For a long time now she had ceased to be Nique except in those letters piling up in a stale-smelling drawer.

Why, she had never noticed on her thighs—she did not think the word *thighs*; one said *legs* from the heels right up to the waist—she had never noticed these thin blue lines that were like rivers on the maps in geography. Wasn't it Aunt Gérardine, her mother's sister, who'd married an engineer in the Ordnance Corps and owned a villa at La Baule, who used to complain of her varicose veins?

She was on the point of crying. No! She would not cry. Why should she cry? It was she who had chosen. She had remained faithful to her vow, faithful to Jacques Améraud.

Yet she no longer believed in it. Or was that true?

It's not possible to peel potatoes and scrape carrots in one's slip. She must get dressed.

But not before she had posted herself behind the window curtain, not before she had cast a long, deep look opposite, where, in the untidy bedroom, in the bedroom redolent of woman, redolent of all the desires of woman, Antoinette had gone back to bed, not beneath the bedclothes but on top of them.

With her head on the pillow, she was reading a book with a yellow cover, holding it up level with her eyes. One leg hung down to the rug, and one hand mechanically caressed her side through the silk.

"What is it, Cécile?"

Cécile wanted to begin doing the room, a job finished in all the other apartments, where bedclothes could be seen airing on the window ledges.

What did Antoinette care?

"Go ahead . . ."

She went on reading. The rugs were shaken around her, things were tidied. Cécile bustled about, small, stiff, and scornful. She would go tell the story to the dragon in the tower. What sort of a life was this?

Antoinette confined herself to changing her place and settling on the couch when at length the bed had to be made.

Dominique had not yet gone down to do her shopping. She still had a headache. She slipped on her darned dress and put on her hat. It was four years old and was of no known fashion. Soon it would be the anonymous hat of an old maid. She looked for her shopping bag.

The air was heavy. Perhaps today the storm would break at last. The sun was without brilliance and veiled, the sky like lead. The concierge was wetting down the entrance. As she passed a little bar a few doors lower down, kept by some people from the Auvergne from whom she bought her wood, there wafted into Dominique's face a strong smell of wine. She heard the dark-faced man talking, with a sonorous accent. In the cellarlike darkness, where the only shining thing was the polished zinc of the counter, she saw some masons chatting, glass in hand, as if time had stayed its course.

She had never looked into a place of this kind, though she had passed this one so often. The picture etched itself on her memory—the smell, the thickness of the air, the bluish shadows in the far corners, the brown of the masons' work jackets, the tint of violet in the bottom of the thick glasses. The mustaches of the man from the Auvergne were lost in the black of the coal dust on his face, in which the whites of his eyes stood out sharply. The sonorities of his voice pursued Dominique through the fiery heat of the street, with its great dead surfaces of gray wall and open windows, and along the melting asphalt under the shattering green-and-white buses, whose conductors pulled at their bells.

She read vaguely: PLACE D'IÉNA.

96

Place d'Iéna? . . . She frowned as she stopped for a moment on the sidewalk. An urchin knocked against her as he ran by. Place d'Iéna? The bus was far away. . . . She gripped her purse tighter. She had been dreaming right on the street. She roused herself, passed from the shade to the sunshine, and went through the door of Sionneau's, to buy a chop.

"Not too thick . . . In the bag . . ."

She avoided the mirrors that pursued her right around the shop, and her gorge rose at the sight of mince on a livid plate running with pink blood.

Part Two

– 6 –

On the rim of the Rond-Point des Champs-Elysées, at the corner of Rue Montaigne, there was a confectioner's shop. The outside of the entire ground floor was faced with a uniform black marble, like a tomb. Three windows stood out, with no surrounding frame, and on the white plush in these windows there was nothing to see except two or three boxes of candy or chocolates, all the same, in mauve and silver.

After that there was nothing. The rest of Rue Montaigne was no more than a kind of canal glistening in the rain between the black walls of buildings. There was nobody, there was nothing, except, nearby, a handcart with its handles in the air, reflected in the wet mirror of the asphalt, and very far off, near Faubourg Saint-Honoré, the rear of a parked taxi.

Rain fell with an unceasing murmur. Great cascades broke loose from cornices, rainspouts emptied at intervals along the sidewalk, and each entryway exhaled icy breath.

For Dominique, Rue Montaigne had, and always

would have, a smell of umbrellas and wet navy-blue serge. She would see herself eternally in the same spot on the left-hand sidewalk, fifty yards from the Rond-Point, in front of a narrow shop window—the only one on the street apart from the confectioner's on the corner—in which there was a display of heaped-up balls of knitting wool.

People ridiculed her, she knew, without any attempt to hide it. From time to time she would lift her nose—slightly too long, slightly crooked—and look calmly at the half-moon windows of the mezzanine floor at number 27.

Four o'clock had struck a short time before. It was November, and not yet night. The gloom that had prevailed all day was growing thicker, and gray was turning to darkness. Only the sky above the street still retained a faint touch of light. Here and there in the buildings lights had been turned on, and two large white globes burned on the mezzanine floor with the half-moon windows, where twenty, twenty-five, perhaps more, girls between fifteen and twenty, all dressed in gray smocks, were at work on cardboard boxes—gluing, folding, passing them from one to another down two long tables. Sometimes they would turn toward the street and burst out laughing as they drew one another's attention to Dominique silhouetted under her umbrella.

It was the fourth, no, the fifth time she had waited here, and who could have believed it was not on her own account that she was waiting? The girls, seeing her stand for a quarter of an hour, for half an hour, and then go away alone, must think that he was not coming, that he never did, never would, come; and that pleased them enormously.

Why today in particular, just as she crossed the Rond-Point, at the very instant when there opened before her the cold wet perspective of Rue Montaigne with its appearance of draining away—had she felt the premonition that it was all over? Now she was almost certain. Had Antoinette felt it too? Why was she still clinging to hope, when it was already twenty past four?

As had happened the last time or two, it was Dominique who had been ready first. She was no longer afraid of feeling embarrassed. She was on her feet, at home, dressed in her navy-blue coat, with her hat and gloves already on, her umbrella on a chair within reach of her hand. Ever since the windows had been permanently shut for the winter, she had had to exercise more attention, sometimes second sight, to understand the comings and goings in the house opposite. But she had come to know it so well!

Antoinette had lunched upstairs with her parents-in-law, as she had been doing since the family had come back from Trouville. She was being nice to them, living almost entirely with them.

Every Wednesday and every Friday she had to invent some pretext. What had she said? That she was going to her mother's, in the big building on Rue Caulaincourt, the windows of which directly overlooked the cemetery? No doubt that was it, because, taking advantage of a moment when Cécile had gone out, she had telephoned, holding her hand in front of her mouth to muffle her voice so as not to be heard upstairs.

"Is that you, Mama? I'm coming to see you this afternoon. In short, you understand. . . . Yes . . . Oh, yes, very happy!" Her smile, however, was somewhat clouded. "Of course, Mama. I'm very careful. . . . Good-bye, Mama . . . One of these days, yes."

At lunch with the Rouets she must have appeared happy. She did everything that was necessary. Often she would spend hours alone with her mother-in-law, as if in payment for the liberty of her Wednesdays and Fridays.

At three-thirty she had not yet gone back downstairs, and only Dominique was ready. Had Madame Rouet tried to keep her? Twenty to four, quarter to four . . . Finally she appeared, in a fever of haste, dressing with hurried, jerky movements, glancing anxiously at the clock, putting on her black silk coat and her silver foxes. On the stairs she must have gone back to get the umbrella she had forgotten.

She was outside. Dominique followed her. She walked along without stopping or turning around, her umbrella tilted a little because of the wind that always blows along the avenue. She was on her way to her Rue Montaigne. Had Rue Montaigne ceased for her, too, as it had for Dominique, to be an ordinary street like any other?

For Dominique, at any rate, that street had a face, a soul, and today that soul had suddenly revealed itself as cold, with something funereal about it.

Very quickly, some twenty yards ahead on the right, Antoinette had turned the handle of a door hidden by a cream-colored curtain, and had gone into a bar over which, too high up, hung a sign on which was painted, in raw white, ENGLISH BAR.

He had not arrived; otherwise they would have come out at once. Dominique had merely glimpsed, very close

104

to the door, the high mahogany counter, the silver tankards, the little flags in the glasses, the red hair of the woman behind the bar.

No one but Antoinette could have powdered her nose mechanically while she confided to her accomplice behind the bar:

"He's late again!"

The little bar was always empty, and so discreet that it could be passed a dozen times without its existence being suspected. Behind the thick curtain there were only three dark tables, at which, it seemed, women like Antoinette must take turns waiting; they were never to be found together.

The minutes passed. The girls in the box-making workroom, under the opaque globes, continued to spy on the waiting Dominique, and commiserated sardonically with her.

Dominique was no longer ashamed for herself; and when, through the window cluttered with balls of wool, an old woman stared too hard at her, she merely took two or three steps under her umbrella, without any attempt not to look like a woman who is waiting.

At the beginning, immediately after Trouville, he had been the first to arrive. The very first time, Antoinette had not had to go inside. He was on watch, holding the door curtain to one side. He had come out, had murmured a few words as he scanned each end of the street. Then he had walked off, while she followed a few paces behind, both of them hugging the wall as they went. A little short of Faubourg Saint-Honoré the man had turned around before he was engulfed in the entrance of a hotel.

The columns by the double swing door were white. An imitation-marble plaque announced: HOTEL DE MONTMORENCY. ALL MODERN CONVENIENCES.

A red carpet could be seen in the lobby, and potted palms. The passerby met blasts of centrally heated air, the stale smell of a hotel frequented by regular clients. Antoinette had entered after him. A little later, a bellhop had drawn the curtains of a second-floor window, a faint light had shown behind the curtains; the rest was silence. There was nothing left in the street except Dominique, making her departure, her throat tight and her skin damp.

The time had soon come when Antoinette walked ahead when they left the little bar. She walked quickly. Out of fear of being met by someone who knew her? Out of shame? Or in order to bury herself the sooner in the warmth of the room with dark red hangings, where she already had her habitual ways of doing things?

Perhaps today she was confiding in the red-haired woman at the *English Bar,* because Antoinette was the kind who can tell their sorrows to another woman— especially to a woman who knows everything and understands everything in that field.

"I thought he would at least leave a note. You're sure there's nothing? . . . The arrangement was that if he was to be detained, he would drop a note here as he went by. . . . Perhaps he telephoned and Angèle took the call? . . ."

She already knew the name of the girl who sometimes took her mistress's place behind the bar.

On the shelves at the back, three or four envelopes were propped between glasses. They bore only first names: Mademoiselle Gisèle, Monsieur Jean . . .

The rain was falling audibly, and sometimes the pattering was louder, the drops rebounding higher from the glistening asphalt. It was growing darker. The light went on in a concierge's lodge, and another light, on an upper floor. Someone approached, but turned in to a doorway before reaching the *English Bar*.

He would not come, Dominique was sure. She was free to go, but she felt she must stay. Her right hand was clenched around the handle of her umbrella. She was very pale in the poor light, and the girls in the box workroom must think she looked ill.

It didn't matter. She was no longer afraid of those eyes peering from the buildings, nor of the lives to be discovered by looking in through doors or windows. Her unruffled demeanor was a challenge. She was not frightened of being taken for a woman in love, for a woman in love about to be left flat. She even took on, involuntarily, the attitude of such a woman, miming her anxiety and jumping when someone came around the corner.

Antoinette was drinking something through a straw, looking at the time by the little clock on the shelf, checking it against her wristwatch.

Four-thirty. Four thirty-five. She had promised herself to wait a quarter of an hour, then half an hour. She decided:

Five minutes more . . .

She powdered her face again and smeared red on her lips.

"If by any chance he should come, you might tell him . . ."

Dominique seemed to sense that she was about to leave, as if invisible bonds linked the two women. She left her post in front of the display of knitting wool and gave a last look at the half-moon windows. Laugh away, young ladies, little fools that you are. He has not come!

Dominique was quite close to the door of the bar when Antoinette came out, in such a state that it was a minute or two before she could manage to open her umbrella.

Their eyes met. At first glance, Antoinette saw just an ordinary woman who happened to be passing. She looked again, as though something had struck her. Had she recognized that face half seen occasionally at a window? Or was she astonished to see in another woman's face the reflection, as it were, of her own? Dominique's dark-ringed eyes seemed to be saying to her:

"He has not come; I know. I foresaw it. He will not come any more."

It lasted only a few seconds. Had it lasted even as long as that? At the corner her hopes rose again. She paused before the mauve-and-silver boxes of the confectioner's. A passing taxi splashed her. She hoped it would stop, but it went on its way, and Antoinette started off again, leaving the deserted street on the far end of which opened the double door of a hotel, with its red carpet and palms, its warmth redolent of bodies undressing behind drawn curtains.

Her gait was jerky. She was about to call a taxi, but changed her mind and turned into the Champs-Elysées. She stopped to let a string of cars go by. There was a large café, an orchestra. She slipped between the tables and reached the downstairs room through a murmur of conversation. On the little tables were cakes, chocolate, silver teapots. There were many women, some of them alone and waiting, as she had been waiting just now. She dropped into a green leather seat in a corner and pushed back her furs with an automatic gesture.

"Tea . . . Writing paper . . ."

Her eyes picked up Dominique, who had sat down not far from her, as though incapable of breaking the spell that joined them. She frowned, trying to remember.

Was she thinking of the two anonymous notes she had received? No. Perhaps she was wondering for a moment whether her mother-in-law was having her followed? Oh no! It wasn't possible. She shrugged her shoulders. It didn't matter. She was pale. She opened her bag and took the cap off a little gold fountain pen. She was about to write. The words had been ready, but now she had lost them, and she looked around with unseeing eyes.

Suddenly she got up and went toward the telephones. After buying a token, she sat briefly in the silence of one of the boxes, where she could be seen through the diamond-shaped window.

Whom had she called? Home? No. More likely a bar he often went to, farther up the Champs-Elysées. She must have asked for him by his first name.

He was not there. She came out to get another token, casting Dominique a glance that showed some impatience.

No! He was not there either. So, letting her tea grow cold, she began to write. She tore up her letter and started again. She must have begun by reproaching him. Now she was imploring, humbling herself too far. It could be read in her face as she acted out her letter. On the point of tears, she tore it up once more. What was needed . . . a brief note, dry, indifferent . . . The pen became sharper, the letters taller. A brief note that would . . .

She lifted her head because a man was passing in front of her, and for one second she had had the insane hope that it was he. This man, too, was tall. He wore the same long overcoat, fashionably cut, the same black felt hat. On the Champs-Elysées there were hundreds of men similarly dressed, who walked in the same way, made the same movements, went to the same barber. But it was not he, not his long pale face and his thin lips with their very private smile.

Why had Dominique, in her mind, called him the Italian? She could have sworn he was Italian. Not the petulant or languishing type, as Italians were commonly represented, but an Italian with a cold exterior and measured gestures.

"Waiter!"

It was an express letter Antoinette had written in the end. She licked the gum with the tip of her tongue.

The waiter, in his turn, called:

"Messenger!"

The room was bright and warm, vibrant with voices, music, and the clash of glasses and saucers. Every face was pink, from the lighting. It was impossible to imagine that rain was falling outside, that Rue Montaigne was looking more and more like a canal, without a soul on the long expanse of shining water, the street lamps coming on one after another along its banks.

Antoinette had nothing more to do, but she couldn't go home so soon. Looking around, she thought she recognized a young woman in brown who was cuddling a little dog on her lap. She began to smile, but the woman looked at her uncomprehendingly. Antoinette realized she had made a mistake, there was only a vague resemblance. She recovered her composure by sipping her tea, which she had forgotten to sugar.

Was she still aware of Dominique's presence, of those eyes staring at her with such burning intensity that she ought surely to feel them? For a long time Antoinette did not turn her way. Then, after a furtive glance, her eyes came back to Dominique, questioning.

She was too badly beaten to be proud.

"Why?" she seemed to be asking. "Why are you here? Why are you the one who appears to be suffering?"

And Dominique shuddered from head to foot. She was living that bitter moment with as much intensity as Antoinette, if not more, savoring the irony of the contrast between the music and the crowd and the expected warmth and intimacy of that second-floor room, the very ordinariness of which was an attraction.

Antoinette had lived through Trouville. One sunny day Dominique had observed that bags were being strapped up on both floors at once. The whole party had left that evening, including Cécile and the old Rouets' maid. The shutters had been closed. For weeks Dominique had had nothing to look at but those closed shutters. She had not even had, close at hand, the echoes of the life of the Cailles, because they, too, had gone away, to spend a few weeks in a little villa the Plissoneaus had rented at Fouras.

The Cailles had sent her a dull, badly printed postcard depicting a handful of wretched huts behind a sand dune, and they had marked a cross over one of them.

She did not know the Rouets' property. She had seen Trouville only once, for a few hours, when she was young and striped bathing suits were still worn. She could not

111

picture it. All she knew was that they were in mourning and accordingly could not join in the lighthearted spirit of vacation time.

For a month Dominique had drifted freely in her solitariness, seized sometimes by such anguish that she had to rub shoulders with the crowd, any crowd, the one in the street or along the Grands Boulevards or in the cinemas. She had never walked so much in her life, until she grew sick of walking—in the sun, past café terraces, along streets as quiet as those in provincial towns, where she peered into the windows, those pockets of shadow in houses.

Off in Trouville, Antoinette, God knows how, had met the Italian. She had been taken there, antagonistic, inert, like a hostage. She had followed her parents-in-law against her will, not daring to oppose them openly, dreaming of the day when she would be free.

And then, when they got back, she might have been their daughter. From the moment of their return, following their habit at Trouville, where they'd lived as one family, she had taken her meals upstairs. They kept house together, so to speak, and when Antoinette did not go upstairs for the afternoon, Madame Rouet went down, her cane innocent of any threat.

Dominique had not needed more than a couple of days to understand how things were. At eleven o'clock each morning she had seen a man walking up and down several times. And behind the window Antoinette's finger had signaled:

"No . . . Not today . . . Not yet . . ."

She had to organize her life in Paris first, she had to warn her mother. The first expedition had been to Rue Caulaincourt. An exuberant, expansive Antoinette, who no doubt threw her hat into the dining room and dropped into an armchair:

"Listen, Mama! I've got some news. . . . I must tell you all about it. . . . If only you knew . . ."

At Rue Caulaincourt you could speak your mind, you could spread yourself, you could behave as you pleased, you could give your moods free rein. It was home. Mother and daughters were of the same breed.

"If only you knew what a man he is! . . . Well, I tread softly, you understand. I flatter the old lady. I spend whole afternoons with her sewing. . . . I must have at least two afternoons free a week. They must think I'm coming to see you. . . ."

She had scoured the shops, buying new clothes, deliberately sober, because of the old lady.

At last, one day her finger behind the window had signaled:

"Yes."

Then it had gone into detail:

"Four . . . four o'clock . . ."

Antoinette had sung. She had remained shut in the bathroom for an hour. She would certainly have appeared too gay at lunch had she not, the better to deceive them, pretended to be depressed.

Now she was about to live. She had begun to live. Body and soul, she was satisfied. She was going to see him, and be alone with him, naked against his nakedness. She was about to live the only life worth living.

Her excitement made her stumble on the curb and forget to look behind her. At the corner of Rue Montaigne she glanced around. She did not yet know the little bar whose address had been given to her. A hand lifted the curtain. The door opened. A man walked ahead, and she followed him, disappearing behind him, swallowed up in the warm lobby of the hotel.

Since then the days had drawn in. The first few times, sunshine still lingered in the streets. Now the lights were on in the buildings. The week before, it had been fully dark when Antoinette came out of the Hotel de Montmorency a minute or two before her companion, and hailed a taxi at the corner to take her the short distance between herself and home.

But it was all over. He would not come any more. Dominique was certain he would not come again. The last time, the two of them had remained for a quarter of an hour in the little bar. Why? Unless he was explaining that he could not stay with her that day, that a business appointment obliged him to be somewhere else, while she must be pleading:

"Just a few minutes . . ."

They sat in the corner close to the window. The bar was so tiny that they had to speak softly. In order not to embarrass them, the proprietress had gone down the spiral staircase leading from behind the bar to the cellar, which had been converted into a kitchen. They whispered, holding hands. The man was embarrassed.

"Just a few minutes!"

She knew she was losing him, but she refused to believe it. He rose.

"Friday?"

"Friday's impossible. I have to take a trip. . . ."

"Wednesday?"

Today was Wednesday, and he had not come. Very soon now, in a bar at the top of the Champs-Elysées, the barman would hand him an express message bearing his first name. He would be with friends and he would say, casually:

"I know what it is."

Perhaps he would stuff the letter into his pocket without reading it.

"Waiter!"

Her hands were damp as she hunted in her bag for change, and her eyes once again fell on Dominique staring at her.

What did Dominique care? Didn't the girls in the box workroom make fun of her? She didn't even pretend to be interested in something else. She was like the little brother and sister she called the poor children when she was six. It was in Orange. Every day, at the same hour, her nursemaid took her out with some toys to the rampart walk. They would settle down on a bench, and invariably the two poor children would come and station themselves two or three yards away, the brother and the sister, ragged, dirty, with scurf in their hair and at the corners of their mouths.

Without the least shame they would stand there, watching her play all by herself. They would not budge. The nursemaid would shout:

"Go and play somewhere else!"

They would merely draw back one step and stand motionless once more.

"Don't go near them, Nique . . . You'll catch little animals."

They heard. Evidently they didn't mind, since they didn't flinch. Finally, the nursemaid, adding action to words, would get up, wave her arms, and, as if scaring sparrows, would go:

"Brr—brr—brr . . ."

It mattered very little that Antoinette shrugged her shoulders scornfully as she passed in front of Dominique. Dominique conveyed her message to her all the same. It was nothing but a look. So much the worse if it was not understood. That look said:

"You see, I know the whole story from the beginning. . . . I didn't understand at first, and I was stupidly malicious. I wrote the two letters to frighten you and keep you from enjoying the results of your crime. . . . I did not yet know you. I did not know that you could not act otherwise. It was life that was driving you on; you needed to live. You did everything for that. . . . You would have gone even further. You went to Trouville with the old dragon from the tower. From a distance you watched people enjoying themselves, who seemed to be living. And, in order to live yourself, you were strong enough to go and eat your meals upstairs, smile at old Madame Rouet, sit opposite her and sew, listen to her interminable reminiscences of her grub of a son. . . .

"Those moments in the little bar, the hours in the Hotel de Montmorency, were enough to pay for all that. You tried to prolong them. You tried to prolong the touch of another's skin against yours; and in the evening, alone in your bed, you would seek, through the odor of your own body, to catch, however faintly, the odor of the man's. . . .

"He did not come today. He will not come again.

"I know. I understand.

"For weeks your windows were shut, and the forbidding brown of the shutters continued the brown of the wall. There was nothing living opposite me, nothing, either, in my apartment. I was alone. I used to put on

116

my hat without looking in the mirror. I used to go down into the street like the poor who own nothing but what some passerby lets fall as he disappears.

"That is the state I have reached.

"He did not come. It's all over. *What are we going to do?*"

For a moment it seemed to Dominique that Antoinette was going to come up and speak to her. They would leave the vast, swarming café together, would plunge side by side into the wet stillness of the night.

"So much effort, so much energy, so much fierce will—only to end in . . ."

Must it all begin again? Must she find another man, other days, no doubt, than Wednesday and Friday, another, but similar, little bar, a hotel to engulf them one after the other?

It was a question now that Dominique's eyes expressed, because Antoinette knew better than she did:

"Is it that?"

Was that what she had been dreaming of on a certain night when she could not sleep and, leaning out of her window in a nightdress, her shoulders white in the moonlight, had contemplated the sky? Was that what she had been thinking of when, with one hand on the doorjamb, she had waited for her husband to die and then entered the room to pour out the medicine on the greenish earth in which the *Phoenix Robelini* was bedded?

Antoinette was suffering. She was suffering so much that, if the man had come in, she could have groveled at his feet there in front of everybody.

Yet Dominique envied her. She had taken for herself, stolen furtively and in passing, a share of it all, the good and the bad. The sight of the little bar had been a blow to her heart. Her skin had become damp as she passed the cream-colored front of the Hotel de Montmorency. What were they going to do now? For Dominique could not imagine that there would be nothing more. Life had to go on.

One behind the other, they took the first street on the right and crossed the lighted rectangle of a cinema as though it were a ditch. The shop windows were brilliantly lighted; the buses, because the street was narrow, scraped the curb; silhouettes crossed one another, brushing against each other. Antoinette turned around impatiently, but behind her, in the cross-hatching of the rain, there was merely an insignificant little body under an umbrella, a commonplace outline, a woman neither old nor young, neither plain nor pretty, not very strong-looking, too pale, the nose rather long and slightly askew—Dominique, walking with hurried steps past the window displays, like any woman going anywhere, moving her lips in the solitude of the crowd.

$$- \, 7 \, -$$

"Cécile! Do you know whether Madame Antoinette has come in?"

"Nearly an hour ago, madame."

"What is she doing?"

"Lying on her bed, fully dressed, with her shoes covered in mud."

"I suppose she's gone to sleep. Go and tell her to come upstairs. The master will be home any minute."

Night was falling early, and the windows were shut, preventing all contact between the wet, cold outer air and the little cubes of warm air forming the cells in which people were preserved. Perhaps because of the thick, yellowish light, the screen made by windows and curtains, and the rain casting a cloak of silence over all movement, the beings in the apartments appeared strangely immobile; and even when they did stir their limbs, they stretched themselves in slow motion, their mute pantomime unrolling itself in a nightmare world where things were in their places for all eternity—a corner of a sideboard, the shine on a piece of chipped crockery, the angle of a half-open door, or the dim perspective of a mirror.

There was no fire in Dominique's flat—nothing to welcome her or make her feel at home except the smell of gas, the odor that hung around longest of all. She was really poor. It was no game that made her reckon her spending in centimes. If there was a game, if she sometimes got to the point of feeling self-satisfied, like those fanatics who practice mortification, it was only an afterthought, an instinctive, unconscious defense—the conversion of cold necessity into a vice in order to make it seem more human. In the square grate there was never more than one log burning at a time, a little log that she made last as long as possible, an operation at which she had become highly skilled. Ten or twenty times, she would alter the angle at which the log lay, letting it char on only one side, then on the other, almost regulating the flame that licked the wood the way you do with a lamp. And before leaving the apartment, she would never fail to put it out. There was now not more than a tiny wave of warmth, and a door opening and closing again was enough to displace it or to dispel it altogether.

A piece of paper rustled on the floor when she came in, and she picked up a letter.

Madame,

I am most distressed at breaking my word to you again—in part at least. I have been twice today to the paper where I am owed money, but the cashier was away. I was faithfully promised he would be back tomorrow. If not, and if these people are really making a fool of me, I shall take other steps.

Please do not think there is any bad faith on my part. As

witness of my good intentions, I enclose something on account, though you will probably think it far too little.

I am writing you this note because we must dine with friends at the other end of Paris, and shall be back very late—perhaps we shall not be back tonight at all. So don't worry about us.

Yours sincerely,
Albert Caille

It was the twentieth of the month. The Cailles had not yet paid their rent. The suitcase had once more left the house—not to fetch Lina's winter coat, but to take away some of the linen from her trousseau. They had gone to sell it on Rue des Blancs-Manteaux.

They owed money at Audebal's and at other shops in the neighborhood, particularly the grocery, since they scarcely ever went to a restaurant now, but would stealthily bring a little food up to their room, though there was still no gas ring there.

When they were alone together, didn't they worry? Albert Caille avoided meeting Dominique, but twice he had sent Lina to her to ask for more time.

Dominique was poorer than they were, because she would be poor always. Tonight she would not eat dinner; her tea at the café on the Champs-Elysées—she had not been able to resist the temptation of a cake on her table—represented more than the cost of one of her usual meals. She would make do with a little warmed-up coffee.

The Cailles had gone to Rue du Mont-Cenis, right at the top of the Butte, in Montmartre, where they now had friends. They were part of a gathering of ten or a dozen in a studio at the back of a courtyard. The women pooled their money and went off to buy cold meat; the men had arranged to bring wine or hard liquor. And in a purposely dim light they relaxed on a broken-down divan or stretched out on the floor, on cushions or a rug, and talked about everything, while the rain, with a desperately slow rhythm, fell on Paris.

Monsieur Rouet got out of a taxi, paid the driver, and gave him twenty-five centimes for a tip. Despite the rain, he had come almost the whole way on foot, under his umbrella, at a regular pace. It was only when he was nearly there that he hailed a cab on Faubourg Saint-Honoré.

Only one half of the double door of the building was open. The light in the hall was yellow; paneling lined the walls to the height of a man; a dark carpet, with brass rods, covered the stairs. The elevator was still at the fifth floor; the fifth-floor tenants always failed to send it down again. He must get the concierge to bring it to their attention once and for all. After all, he owned the building. He waited, took his place in the narrow cage, pushed the button.

The bell rang far away in his apartment. Cécile opened the door, took his hat and wet umbrella, and helped him out of his black overcoat. A few minutes later, the three family members were seated at the table in the dark-furnished dining room, under the unchanging light of the chandelier.

Their surroundings seemed eternal. Furniture and ornaments gave the appearance of having always existed there, and of pursuing their solemn life without heed of the three people wielding spoon and fork, or of Cécile gliding noiselessly about in her felt slippers.

Then, when the second course was being served and

only sighs were to be heard, Antoinette had a fit of absence. As she raised her head, as she perceived the aged faces on her left and right, her eyes expressed a terrified stupor. It was as if she were seeing for the first time the world that surrounded her. She was like someone waking in an unknown house. These two beings, although so familiar, who hemmed her in like jailers—she did not know them, they were nothing to her, no bond linked them to her, she had no reason for being there, for breathing the same air as these two worn-out souls or for sharing their threatening silence.

From time to time Madame Rouet would look at her, and her look was never indifferent; her slightest word always had a meaning.

"Are you ill?"

"I don't feel very well. I've been to my mother's. I decided to walk down Rue Caulaincourt, and there was a gusty wind. Perhaps I've caught a chill."

Madame Rouet must know that she had been crying: her eyelids were still burning and sore.

"Did you go to the cemetery?"

She did not understand at once.

"No . . . not today . . . It was when I got to my mother's that I felt tired and began to shiver. . . ."

Her eyes were filling. She could have cried there, at the dinner table, if she had not made an effort. Yet just then her crying would have been without cause; she was not thinking of the man who had not come. She was simply generally unhappy, for every reason and for none.

"You must take a hot drink and a couple of aspirin before you go to bed."

Anyone examining the walls could have read there

the whole history of the Rouet family. He would have found, among others, a photograph of Madame Rouet as a girl, dressed for tennis, racquet in hand; and, oddly enough, she was slender—really a girl.

Farther along, in a black frame, was Monsieur Rouet's engineering diploma and, by way of pendant to it, his father-in-law's factory at the time he had entered it at twenty-four years of age.

He had worn his hair *en brosse* and very correct clothes, with no style, such as he was to wear all his life—the clothes of a man who works, for whom every hour is dedicated to work.

Had any other man worked as hard as he had?

A photograph of the wedding: at twenty-eight, the engineer had married his boss's daughter. Everyone, though imbued with tranquil happiness, was serious and had a dignity nothing could touch, as in a pious illustration. The workers had sent a delegation. They had been given a banquet in one of the factory shops.

It was still only a small factory. The big one, the one Rouet had sold some years ago for many millions, was created by him, and he had carried the whole burden on his shoulders day by day, minute by minute. Yet in his eyes, as in hers, had not his wife always remained his boss's daughter?

"Were you out of the office this afternoon, Germain?"

It was a man of sixty-six she had before her. He had remained as tall, as broad, as upright as ever. His hair, though it had turned white, had remained as wiry. Yet he had given a start, and he hesitated before giving an answer. He knew that every one of his wife's words had a meaning.

"I had so much to do that I don't remember now.

. . . Wait a minute . . . There was a moment when Bronstein . . . No . . . I don't think I left the office. Why do you ask?"

"Because I telephoned at five o'clock and you weren't there."

"You're quite right. . . . At five o'clock I saw a client, Monsieur Michel, down to the corner. I wanted to say a few words to him out of Bronstein's hearing."

Perhaps she believed him, perhaps not. More probably not. Soon, after letting him go to bed first, she would search his wallet and count the notes in it.

He showed not the slightest bad temper, but went on eating calmly and serenely. It had been such a long time! He had never rebelled; he never would rebel. His body was like a husk that people think has nothing in it, because he had accustomed himself to keep everything bottled up inside. Even inside there was no rebellion now, scarcely even bitterness. He had worked so very, very hard. He had worked so hard that the mass of work, the mountain of human labor at his back, bore him down, frightening him, like the eiderdown that, in a nightmare, threatens to fill the whole room.

He had had a son. Probably, surely, the son of his body, but he had never felt there was anything in common between them. He had vaguely watched the boy grow without being able to take any interest in the formless sickly being. He had put him into one office after another. Then, since he had sold his business and the doctor ordered rest, he had placed his son, like an ornament, with a suitable title, in a business in which he had an interest, a business involved with safes.

The light modeled each of the three faces differently as they ate and breathed. Cécile watched maliciously from the door for the moment to change the plates, and she seemed to hate all three equally.

In a bar on the Champs-Elysées there was doubtless a tall man, faultlessly dressed and pale-faced, drinking cocktails while he looked through the racing papers, scarcely remembering Rue Montaigne.

Young men and women with the whole of life before them drank and talked excitedly in the dim studio on Rue du Mont-Cenis, and Dominique, close to the log whose tiny flame kept her company, reached mechanically for the stocking basket. With bent head, she threaded her wool and slipped the varnished wooden egg into a gray stocking whose foot was already so darned that now she was darning nothing but old darns. She was not hungry. She had trained herself not to be hungry. We are assured that the stomach grows used to this and becomes quite small. She must have a minute stomach, for next to nothing was enough for her.

Silence rose from the black and shining street; it oozed from the apartments, from the windows with drawn curtains behind which people were breathing; silence dripped off the walls; and the unvarying patter of the rain was a form of silence, too, since it rendered the void more palpable.

It had been raining like that—only the rain was more continuous and harder, with sudden gusts that did their best to blow umbrellas inside out—when one evening she had chanced to go along Rue Coquillière, near the markets. She'd been to buy buttons to match an old dress she'd had dyed. On the sides of the gaping doorways were rows of brass or enamel plates, with many strange names and professions and businesses. There were dark and rickety staircases; there were fruit baskets in the shelter of entrances and swarming blackness that smelled of the oil in which a street seller, in the full blast of the wind, was frying potatoes.

From one of these doorways Dominique had seen Monsieur Rouet emerge. She had never suspected that this was the sort of place he went off to each morning with his dignified and measured step, like a clerk going to his office. How did he cross these slimy streets without dirtying his always spotless shoes? It was his form of dandyism. From time to time he would look down to make sure there was no splash of mud to make a little star on the gleaming black of the patent leather.

SOCIÉTÉ PRIMA

ARTICLES DE PARIS

STAIRCASE B, ENTRESOL,

END OF THE CORRIDOR ON THE LEFT

On the pallid enamel plate a black hand pointed the way.

In gray rooms with splintered floors on the entresol, where your head brushed against the ceiling and the paper moldered on the walls, there were goods in every corner—cases, bales, cardboard boxes; blue and green combs, Bakelite powder boxes, things shiny, nickeled, varnished, vulgar, badly made, things that are sold in bazaars and at fairs. A fifty-year-old woman in a black smock sorted them from morning till night and received clients. One door was always shut. It was knocked on only in fear and trembling. Behind it, at a light wooden desk, and with a huge safe at his back, sat Monsieur Bronstein, his skull naked and gleaming except for a single lock of black hair, which seemed to have been drawn on with India ink.

127

On the left side of the office was a single armchair, worn but comfortable. Beyond it were a small sink, a scrap of soap, and a red-bordered towel with a musty smell.

It was here, in this armchair, that Monsieur Rouet settled himself after crossing, without a glance, the rooms cluttered with shoddy goods.

"Nobody here?"

If there was a client with Monsieur Bronstein, he would slip into a little storeroom, where he would wait standing, as men wait behind a door or a screen in houses of ill repute where the clients never meet one another.

Société Prima was his business. This was what he had invested his millions in, and Bronstein made them fruitful. The *articles de Paris* were a façade; the true activity of the business resided entirely in the huge, inappropriate safe, crammed with bills, IOUs, and strange contracts.

It was here, facing Monsieur Bronstein, that small-business men in difficulties, skilled workmen, embarrassed manufacturers came to their doom. They would enter with a constrained smile, determined to bluff and lie, and a few minutes later they would have vomited the whole dirty truth. They were nothing but men in desperate straits, who could have been made to kneel down before the safe, its door deliberately left ajar.

When it was not raining, Monsieur Rouet would sometimes, for his health, traverse the distance between Rue Coquillière and Faubourg Saint-Honoré at his usual even pace, skirting the turbulent sea of life; and some who saw him going by, always at the same hour, admired him for a spry old gentleman.

Dominique, without wanting to, had followed him

elsewhere, on more troubling wanderings. She had seen him camouflaged under his umbrella, slipping with hunched shoulders into the alleys in the neighborhood of the markets. She had seen him walk with a different step, irregular and uncertain, toward a distant silhouette under a lamp, slow, then turn around to start off in a different direction. She had not at first understood the meaning of this chase. She had been oppressed by the chaotic streets, the icy black doorways, the staircases opening straight off the street, the frosted globes over the doors of mysterious hotels, and the shadows in the windows of little bars where people awaited God knows what, immobile as waxworks.

The man of the wire factory, the man of Faubourg Saint-Honoré, of the table set in the unchanging dining room, went on as though driven by an implacable force. His walk became that of an old man, and he brushed past girls who came out of the shadows to accost him. Their faces, as though magnetically attracted, loomed up for a moment in the uncertain light, and he would set off again, bowed down and anxious, gnawing at his fever, hovering between hope and despair.

Dominique finally understood. At the corner of an alley, she had seen him stop near a thin little girl with no hat and wearing a sorry green coat like a cloak over her shoulders. She was walking less confidently than the others, no doubt because she was underage. She had looked up with a shake of her damp hair, as if to give him a better chance to look her over, and he had followed a few paces behind, just as Antoinette, on Rue Montaigne, had followed the Italian. He had plunged in her wake into one of those doorless openings, where his feet had stumbled on the treads of a staircase. A light had gleamed, and Dominique had fled in terror. She had wandered around for a long time in anguished fear of not being able to escape from this dreadful labyrinth.

Now, across the street, they were eating dessert, all three of them, under the chandelier. Each was thinking his own thoughts, following their simple or complicated thread; only Madame Rouet looked at the others, as if she alone bore the burden of their lives and the life of the whole building.

On the wall in front of her hung a portrait of her son at five or six, with a straw hat on his head and a hoop in his hands. Was she the only one who had failed to realize even then that he was not an ordinary boy, but a spoiled sample—a vague, erratic creature? Then there was the other photograph, of her son as a young man, trying to put on a bold face and looking straight ahead. But wasn't it clear that he would never achieve a normal life, that nothing would drag him out of his incurable melancholia?

The only relic he had left in the house was Antoinette, the stranger with whom there was no point of contact, she who, now that her husband was dead, sat at their table instead of continuing her own life, with her mother on Rue Caulaincourt or some such place.

From outside, all this came to nothing more than curtains with a faint light throbbing behind them. In the dining room, in the very heart of the Rouet family, the whole of life was concentrated in the old lady's terribly clear-sighted eyes, resting without emotion, without love on the others' faces—on the false serenity of her husband's face, or on her daughter-in-law's, flushed with youth.

She knew everything. It was she who had dictated

the marriage settlement. It was she who, from the very first years, had created the life of the family, had channeled it and banked it. It was she who had prevented her son from having a life of his own, who had wanted him to remain a child all his life, even in his work, in which he was no more than a clerk at the factory.

It was she who, since she could not prevent his marriage, had attached the second household to her own; and it was because of her that the young couple had had nothing of their own, but depended entirely on their monthly allowance and such odd sums as she doled out to them.

A cold smile played on her lips when her eyes fell momentarily on Antoinette's shoulders, on that young, ardent flesh quivering with the urge to escape.

Antoinette owned nothing but her furniture. Before she had any money under her own control, she would have to wait till her parents-in-law were dead; and even then she would enjoy only the interest on the fortune, which at her death would revert to distant Rouet relatives, or, more likely, to some of the Leprons.

That was as it should be. That was why Antoinette stayed on in the house, why she had gone to Trouville, why, for fear of being poor, she went upstairs to eat her meals with them, and why, for hours at a time, she kept her mother-in-law company.

"You've scarcely eaten a thing."

"I'm not hungry. I'm sorry."

Antoinette was afraid she would not reach the end of dinner without breaking down. She would have liked to shriek, to bite, to cry out her hurt, to call the man who had not come, like a creature of the woods tragically calling its mate.

131

"You look as though you've been crying."

And Cécile, by the door, feasted on each thrust.

"Mother and I talked about some depressing things."

"About Hubert, was it?"

Antoinette was so far away that involuntarily she raised her eyes in astonishment.

Hubert? She remembered so little of him. She could scarcely have called up his face with her eyes shut. He was dead, quite dead. There was nothing left of him but a confused picture, an impression of sadness, of a dreary existence dragging on and threatening to last forever.

"One day, when it's not raining, we'll go and visit the grave together. Won't we, Antoinette?"

"Yes, Mama."

She was not sure she had spoken. Her voice had passed into the air like someone else's. She felt she must get up and release the tension.

"I beg your pardon . . ."

She saw the two sitting opposite each other. She did her best to convince herself that it was she—Antoinette—who was there. She repeated:

"I beg your pardon . . ."

She fled. She had a mad longing to go out into the damp night, to scour the Champs-Elysées, to hunt for him in every bar, to cry out to him that it was impossible, that he could not abandon her, that she would do anything, that she would take up hardly any room, if only he . . .

"Cécile! Go downstairs with Madame Antoinette. I think she's not well."

Then Monsieur Rouet said, as he hunted in his pocket for a toothpick:

"What's the matter with her?"

"You wouldn't understand."

The truth was, she herself did not know yet, but she would find out, she was sure. Her sole object in life was to find out everything that went on around her in the circle she dominated.

"Being alone is doing her no good. It's odd that she hasn't a single woman friend."

How like a man to say that! Words, words! Did the Rouets have friends? They did not even see the more or less close relatives whom they had left scattered along their path and who used to write humbly to them at the new year because they were rich.

Women friends—what for? Was it likely that Madame Rouet would allow strangers, men or women, to invade her house?

True, one had had to be admitted: Antoinette herself. Because her son had wanted her, no matter what it cost, because, weak as he was, he could let his desire make him ill.

"You shall have your wife!"

He had got her. Then he found out what it meant. He soon grew tired of following wherever she hurried, driven by her need to keep moving, to circle around the bright lights.

"Admit you're not happy."

"But I am, Mama!"

Then why had he started collecting stamps, and begun learning Spanish next, all by himself, for whole evenings at a time?

Now, Antoinette was going quietly. Madame Rouet had broken her in.

"Tell Madame Antoinette to come up."

She came up.

"Antoinette, hand me the blue thread. Not that one. The navy blue. Now thread my needle . . ."

She quivered, she trembled with impatience, but she obeyed. She stayed there for hours, under the shadow of her mother-in-law.

"Hm! You've been crying! . . . Hm! You weren't hungry. . . ."

If only she had been able to walk like other people! What a paradox it was to have a brain so keenly alive, a mind so agile and clear, a will so fierce, and to have to drag around a pair of legs that were slowly turning into pillars of stone!

She struggled. When she was alone, when no one could take her unawares, she would get up unaided, at the price of painful effort, and would force herself to walk around the room, deliberately dispensing with her cane, counting the steps. She *would* manage somehow, she *would* achieve mastery over these accursed legs. But nobody need know.

It was not to Rue Caulaincourt that Antoinette had gone to revel in sad thoughts. Madame Rouet's lips pushed forward in a contemptuous sneer. She knew them—the sort of people whose only desires were trivial and whose only thoughts were how to satisfy them.

Antoinette's mother was of that kind. It was certain that her daughter slipped money to her on the sly, and that each note was converted into an immediate pleasure—a lobster, dinner at a restaurant, a visit to the cinema, neighboring women asked in for coffee and cake, or some frightful dress she would buy herself after spending a whole day in the big stores.

"My daughter who married the Rouets' son . . . The Rouet wire factory, you know . . . A family with millions, yet they live like the most ordinary people. When she got married, they didn't even have a car! It was she who . . ."

The woman was almost equally proud of her other daughter, Colette, who was kept by a brewer from the north. She would visit her in her apartment in Passy, hiding in the kitchen when the fifty-year-old brewer turned up unexpectedly. Perhaps she listened—she was certainly capable of listening without shame—to the noises they made in the bedroom or the bathroom.

"Hand me my glasses, Félicie. Hasn't Cécile come up?"

A voice from the hall.

"Here I am, madame."

"What is she doing?"

"At first she wouldn't let me turn down the bed. She told me to go away. She shouted:

" 'Please leave me alone! Can't you see that . . .' "

And Madame Rouet's unchanging voice:

"Then what?"

"Nothing. She didn't finish. She shut herself up in the bathroom. I did the bed. When I left, she was crying. You could hear her through the door from a dozen yards away."

"Hand me my glasses."

At midnight Antoinette's mother came out of a cinema on the Place Blanche with a neighbor from the same floor, whom she had treated. There were still the temptations of the brightly lighted brasseries, of a little extra pleasure.

"Let's stand ourselves a liqueur at Graff's?"

135

Motionless in his bed, Monsieur Rouet waited for sleep, waited for nothing else: he had long since accepted the bounds of his life.

Dominique was darning gray stockings. All the stockings in the basket were gray. She never wore any other kind; they showed the dirt least. She was convinced that they were the strongest and that they went with any dress.

From time to time she would raise her head, making out the white pearls on the windowpanes, a touch of diffused pink behind the windows opposite, and nothing but black on the floor above. Then she would bend over her work again, reaching out to give a gentle turn to the log in order to keep the yellow flame alive.

She was the last one in the street to go to bed. The Cailles had not come home. She waited for them a little longer in the silence, went to sleep, rose before dawn, and watched the windowpanes grow pale, but the couple did not get back until seven in the morning, after trailing around the markets among the damp vegetables and the vagrants sheltering in doorways.

Both had drawn faces, particularly Albert, who had had too much to drink. For fear of meeting their landlady, they turned the key in the lock noiselessly and crossed the living room on tiptoe.

Lina asked in a tired voice:

"What do we do now?"

"First of all, we're going to sleep."

They did not make love when they went to bed, but only toward midday, when they were half awake, and then they went to sleep again. It was two o'clock when the sound of water was heard in the bathroom.

Antoinette had gone out at ten in the morning and

had not reappeared in Faubourg Saint-Honoré, but she must have telephoned. Toward noon Madame Rouet had walked slowly to the telephone, and only two places had been laid for lunch.

Now, Monsieur Rouet, punctual as ever, was leaving the house and making his way to Rue Coquillière.

— 8 —

The train. As it left the station, puffing its smoke between swaying lines of houses, crusts of snow could still be seen in sheltered corners on the black of the embankments, for night had not quite fallen.

The last time, in August, it had been Antoinette who went off, leaving Dominique alone in Paris for long, weary weeks. Today, it was Dominique who was in the train, still standing for a moment in the corridor before entering her third-class compartment.

She had only just received the telegram: AUNT CLÉMENTINE PASSED AWAY. FUNERAL WEDNESDAY. FRANÇOIS.

She did not understand, for today was Tuesday. The death must have occurred on Sunday, since burial usually takes place three days after death. Unless it had been a particularly contagious illness? But Aunt Clémentine had not died of a contagious illness. She must be . . . let's see . . . seventy-four and seven . . . eighty-one. The weather was not warm. Even in Toulon it was not warm in January, and there was no need to hurry the interment.

Which Francois? The father, François de Chaillou, who would have been in Rennes? Or wasn't it more probably his son, who had joined the navy? The son, without a doubt. That made more sense. Aunt Clémentine had lived alone, with a maid even older than she was, in her villa near the railroad crossing at La Seyne-sur-Mer, where Dominique had sometimes spent her vacations. If she had been ill for a long time, some member of the family would have gone to her and would have written to Dominique. It must have been very sudden. François had been informed because he was the nearest. It was François who had sent out the telegrams, and he must have forgotten his cousin. Yes, that was how it had happened. She was always being forgotten. She counted so little!

Antoinette would perhaps not notice her absence. She would see closed shutters for three or four days without wondering what had happened to her neighbor. The Cailles were being left alone in the apartment. It was to be hoped they would not take advantage of the fact to invite their friends from Rue du Mont-Cenis and spend the entire night drinking and carrying on with them in the living room.

The train compartment was full. Dominique had a seat next to the window. Beside her was a sailor returning from leave, and there was another opposite. Without enthusiasm they exchanged allusions to their stay in Paris, winks, and occasional words about mates they would soon be seeing again. It was clear that, like brothers, there was no reserve between them. They soon dropped off to sleep, their berets over their eyes. The one next to Dominique bumped into her from time to time and leaned against her with all his weight on the curves.

For a long time she thought idly, looking at the sailor opposite and then at a woman feeding her baby. The woman's great white breast made her feel sick. A railroad clerk was reading a cheap novel. The noise of the train gradually penetrated her head, and its rhythm overlaid that of her breathing and the beating of her heart. She relaxed. An icy draft from the window played on the nape of her neck. Her feet were on the metal plate of the heating apparatus, which gave off steam. She closed her eyes, then opened them again. Someone turned the electric switch, reducing the light to a blue glimmer. It was warm, but the draft still felt like a thin jet of cold water. Dominique's eyelids pricked. The train stopped, people moved off to the obscurity of a station, lights glided by, and the train was in motion again. They must have gone a long way, past Dijon, when she saw that someone was chasing the train in the pale light of the haloed moon.

She was not astonished. She simply said:

"Why, Madame Augustine!"

And she gave a gentle, sad smile, such as people exchange who know each other's misfortunes. She understood, all of a sudden. It was a full week since she had last seen Mademoiselle Augustine at her window, but two or three times she had caught a glimpse of the concierge up in the attic.

The old spinster was dead, like Aunt Clémentine. She was happy to be dead, and was running after the train. Finally she reached Dominique's compartment, and sat down beside her, a little out of breath, smiling and delighted, though with a touch of embarrassment, because she was not a pushy sort of person.

It was odd to see her thus, milky and almost luminous, so attractive, so beautiful—because she *was* beautiful, and yet she could be recognized!

She stammered, appealingly bashful:

"I nearly missed you. I went to your apartment as quickly as I could; the thing was still warm on my bed. I had always promised to keep my first visit for you, but you had just left. So I rushed to the Gare de Lyon . . ."

Her breasts, which formerly seemed like jellyfish, stood up firmly.

"I'm so happy! But understand, I'm not used to it yet. The concierge is up there laying it out; she thoroughly enjoys washing a dead woman and moving her around . . ."

Dominique could very well picture the concierge, a skinny woman slowly dying of TB, who laid out all the corpses in the neighborhood.

"She went knocking on the doors, shouting:

" 'She's dead! Madame Augustine is dead!'

"And I, I left on tiptoe. . . . I've been waiting so long. I thought it would never come! In the end I was suffocating. I was too hot in that great body. Did you notice that I perspired a lot and that my perspiration had a strong smell? I used to look at you from the distance. I knew you were looking at me too. You were saying to yourself:

" 'Look! Old Augustine is at her window. . . .'

"And I wanted so badly to fly across to you and tell

you everything! . . . But you wouldn't have understood. . . . Now, it's all over. I am at peace. I'm going to keep you company to the end of your journey."

Dominique felt a hand endowed with unearthly warmth and life clasping hers. She was as much moved as at the first touch of her loved one's hand. She felt a little embarrassed. She, too, had not been used to it, and she turned her head away with a blush.

"Admit it," stammered Madame Augustine. "I was a hideous old maid. . . ."

Dominique wanted to say no, out of politeness, but she knew it was impossible from now on to lie to her.

"Yes! Yes! . . . It distressed me, I can tell you! . . . I was so glad when I finally caught pneumonia. They cupped me, and I had to let them do it. . . . There were moments when I thought they were going to save me, but I took advantage of an hour when they left me alone. . . .

"I love you so much!"

Dominique was not shocked. This love was not ridiculous. It seemed to her to be quite natural, to be what she had always been waiting for.

Her only embarrassment was on account of the two sailors. She wanted to tell Madame Augustine about them; perhaps she had not seen them. But her will was growing numb and a supernatural lassitude was taking hold of her. She was warm to the very depths of her flesh, her veins, her bones. An arm twined around her, lips drew close to hers; she closed her eyes, panting. A unique sensation stiffened her whole being; she was afraid, she was sinking, she . . .

———

Dominique never knew whether she had really moaned. In the pale blue half-darkness of the compartment she saw nothing but the eyes of the sailor opposite staring at her. Perhaps he had just waked up? Or had he been floating between waking and sleeping for a long time?

She was uneasy again, and ashamed. Something had almost happened inside her and then stopped short— something that filled her with foreboding, frightened her, something she dared not give a name.

She did not sleep for the rest of the night. With the first glimmerings of dawn, when they had just passed Montélimar, she stood in the corridor, her face motionless against a window, watching the first olive trees go by, the red, almost flat roofs, and the white houses.

The sun was shining at Saint-Charles, and she went to the station buffet for a cup of coffee and a croissant, keeping an eye all the time on her train.

Farther on she caught glimpses of the sea. It was very blue, with an infinity of white crests, for the mistral was blowing. The sky was clear, but on the road people could be seen holding their hats on.

At Toulon she took the streetcar. Despite her shame, she had not succeeded in altogether dispelling the extraordinary sensation that still lingered in the most secret recesses of her being.

It had happened to her just once before, a long time ago, when she was sixteen or seventeen; but then the sensation had opened out like a rocket in the deep blue of the sky, leaving her dazed and hollow.

In an open taxi she recognized her cousin Bernard, with a girl she had never seen. She waved to them, but

Bernard turned around too late, and the streetcar was too far behind.

"My poor Nique! How tired you must be. Go upstairs for a minute and freshen yourself."

The burial was to take place in an hour's time. The house was full of uncles, aunts, and cousins. They all kissed her.

"You're always the same!" they said. "What time did you get François's telegram? Just imagine, he didn't have your address. So you've arrived too late to see *her* for the last time. We couldn't wait too long, you understand. . . ."

Then, in a whisper: "She was beginning to smell."

Her legs had swollen lately. . . . Oh, no, she hadn't changed. If Dominique had been able to see her . . . She looked as if she was asleep. . . . Did she remember that the little Cottron boy said one day, in his childish way, that Aunt Clémentine tasted of preserved fruit. . . . Ah, well! she stayed like that right to the end . . . but . . .

"Go and wash . . . You'll hear everything soon. . . . You'll be very surprised! . . . Have you seen poor old Uncle François? . . . He *would* come, just the same. . . . Oh, dear! We're very much afraid that it'll be his turn one of these days, and that we'll all be meeting again soon, in Rennes. . . ."

There were a great many people at the funeral, a great many uniforms. The women's veils floated out. They had gone over the tracks before Dominique had even noticed them. Everything seemed smaller to her, the villa, too, and so commonplace!

Several times during the service she thought of Antoinette, seeing her again, at another funeral, in Saint-

Philippe-du-Roule. As they left the cemetery, she found herself once more surrounded by the entire family. And her uncles and aunts had become old people.

"*You* haven't changed!"

They had. So had her cousins—mature persons now, married and parents themselves.

She was introduced to a boy of thirteen, who said:

"How d'you do, Aunt."

"It's Jean's son."

What she was most astonished to rediscover was the vocabulary of long ago—those words that were meaningless outside the family, the clan. Sometimes she had to make an effort to understand.

Two big tables had been set in the dining room and the living room of the villa. All the children had been put at one table. Beside her there was a Polytechnic student in uniform. He had a bass voice and continually addressed her as "Little Aunt."

"The math prof is a wizard type. . . ."

"I'm doing lang and lit. . . ."

The same fetish-words, uttered by creatures she had known as babies, or of whose existence she knew only from New Year letters.

"Berthe Babarit, who married an officer in the Engineers last year, has just had a baby. . . ."

She watched them. She felt that they were covertly watching her, too, and it embarrassed her. She would have liked to be like them, to feel once more that she belonged to the clan. They were at ease, talked as though they had never parted. Some, who lived in the same town and often met, alluded to common friends, to details of careers and to vacations spent at the seaside together.

"Don't you feel too much alone in Paris, Nique? I've always wondered why you stayed in that big city, when . . ."

"I'm quite happy."

Nique hasn't changed! Nique hasn't changed! They repeated it to her as if she alone of the whole family had always been the same age, forty, as if she had always been an old maid.

Yes, they had expected her not to marry, and they found it quite natural. Nobody referred to the possibility of another kind of life.

"I wonder how Aunt Clémentine could do such a thing. If she had been in need, that would at least have been an excuse! But she was drawing a pension. She had everything she needed. . . ."

"She who was so affectionate, and loved children so!"

An aunt cut in:

"You only really love children when you have your own. Anything beyond, believe me, is just affectation. . . ."

Aunt Clémentine's real victim was Dominique, who said nothing, and did her best to maintain the slightly mournful smile that she got from her family, that she had always seen on her mother's and her aunts' faces.

There had been only one person from whom she had a chance of eventually inheriting anything—Aunt Clémentine—and now they'd told her that Aunt Clémentine, without a word to a soul, had put all her property into an annuity.

There was nothing left except some personal ornaments, a little box of old jewels, and some knickknacks, because the furniture had been willed to the old maid, Emma, whom they had tried to get to sit down with the family, but she'd insisted on remaining alone in the kitchen.

"What would you like to have as a memento, Nique? I was saying to Uncle François that the cameo would please you. It's a little old-fashioned, but it's very beautiful. Aunt Clémentine wore it right up to the end."

Certain groups were going home by train that day, so the division of what was left began at four o'clock.

The children were sent out into the garden. There was a debate over the two wedding rings, for Aunt Clémentine, who had been a widow, had worn two. They had been removed from her body after death, and there were some who said that was wrong.

"Let's give the earrings to Céline and the watch to Jean . . ."

The men talked shop. Those with army ties or government service discussed the merits of posts in the colonies.

"Fortunately, we have a very good school. I don't want to be promoted for at least three years, until the children have passed their bachot. It's always a bad thing to change teachers. . . ."

"Nique! The cameo? Really and truly?"

And she murmured automatically, because it was what she was expected to say:

"It's too much!"

"Oh no! Come on! You'd better take this photograph as well, of you in the garden with Aunt Clémentine and her husband. . . ."

A shed had since been put up opposite the house, so only a tiny bit of the sea was visible now.

"Why don't you come and spend a few days with us at Saint-Malo? It would give you a change. . . ."

Did they think she needed a change? No! These were the words they spoke every time they met. Invitations were issued and then never referred to again.

"When do you go back?"

"Tomorrow."

"You've reserved a room at a hotel? Here, you understand . . . We could all have dinner together this evening in a restaurant. . . . François, where could we have dinner—not too expensive?"

They kissed again. Occasionally Dominique felt that contact was on the point of being made, and that she would once more be part of the clan. Her uneasiness turned into anguish. All these faces revolved around her, running into one another, standing out suddenly with a stupefying clarity, and she said to herself:

"It's So-and-so!"

She was too exhausted to go back by the night train, and she managed, with some difficulty, to find a room in a tiny hotel pervaded by an indefinably hostile smell, which kept her from sleeping almost all night.

She left by the morning train, alone, with the cameo in her handbag. A slanting sun came into the compartment, in which, for many long hours, there was the noisy coming and going of passengers making short journeys. On the outskirts of Lyons the sky became white, then turned gray, and the first flakes of snow were to be seen above Chalon-sur-Saône. Dominique ate sandwiches she had bought at the station. Then, the rest of the way to Paris, she existed as though in a tunnel, her eyes half closed, her features drawn and etched deep by fatigue and the feeling of emptiness, of uselessness, she had brought away from Toulon.

When she reached Rue du Faubourg Saint-Honoré,

she was annoyed to find no one in. The Cailles were not there. Perhaps they would not come back until the early hours. The room was cold; there was no odor. She lighted a log before she took off her coat, and held a match over the gas ring.

The shutters of old Augustine's window were closed. She never used to close her shutters. So she really was dead.

There was no light in Antoinette's apartment. It was ten o'clock. Should Dominique really believe that she'd already gone to bed? No! She could sense an emptiness behind the curtained windows.

Only on the floor above did a little light come through, yellow light that moved from the dining room to the bedroom, and near eleven o'clock went out. Antoinette was not with her parents-in-law either.

Dominique readied her bed, unpacked her bag carefully, and gazed at the cameo before shutting it up in the drawer in which she kept her mementos, all the while looking out the window frequently, cross and irritated that Antoinette had taken advantage of her absence to begin a new life.

It was January now. For more than a month nothing had happened. Once or twice a week Antoinette had gone to visit her mother on Rue Caulaincourt. One day, about five o'clock, the two women had gone together to the cinema. Afterward, they'd met Colette in a café on one of the Grands Boulevards.

For two weeks more Antoinette had furtively gone into the little bar on Rue Montaigne. She was well aware that it was futile, and merely stopped in and then left.

"Nothing for me?"

"Nothing, madame."

She had grown thin and pale, and was once more spending hours reading, stretched out on her bed, and smoking.

Several times her eye had caught Dominique's, and this was not the hasty glance you bestow on a passerby: her eyes were insistent. Antoinette knew that Dominique knew everything, and there was a question in her wide eyes:

Why?

She could not figure her out. It was not mere curiosity she divined in this unknown woman who followed her so closely.

Sometimes it was as though a sort of affection, of trust even, was about to spring up.

You who know everything . . .

But they did not become acquainted. They continued passing, each going her own way, carrying her own thoughts with her.

Antoinette was not ill and she had not gone to bed, but it did not occur to Dominique that she could simply have gone to the cinema.

No! At this time of night people were coming out of the cinemas. People could be heard coming home; taxis tore along at full speed; the last buses lumbered along the streets; flakes of snow fell slowly and on the spot where they came to rest on the cold stones there was nothing left a few seconds later.

Ten times Dominique gazed at the closed shutters of Augustine's attic, and each time she was overwhelmed with shame. She could not understand how she could have had such a dream, and yet she knew it was not a product of chance. She did not want to think of it, yet she was tempted to decipher its deep meaning.

Was she another Augustine? The villa at Toulon came to her mind's eye again. The relatives she had known as uncles and aunts had grown old or were dead. Those she had known as children were now adults in their turn—the girls were mothers, the wild schoolboys were engineers or magistrates, the babies talked of math and lang and lit, and called her Aunt Dominique.

"You haven't changed, Nique!"

They said it in all sincerity. Because her life had not changed. Because nothing in particular had happened to her.

Old Augustine was dead. Tomorrow or the day after she would be buried, as Aunt Clémentine had been buried.

Then there would be no old maid left in the street. Or . . . now it was Dominique's turn.

She was floundering. She went to look at herself in the mirror. It wasn't true that she was old! It wasn't true that life was over for her. Her flesh had not withered. Her skin had remained white and soft. Under her eyelids there might be a tiny line, a fairly deep one, but it could scarcely be seen. It was a matter of temperament and health—as a girl, she had been given tonics and injections.

As for her body, which she alone knew, it was that of a girl and without blemish.

Why did Antoinette not come home? The last bus had gone by, and it was past time for the last Métro train.

It was treachery to take advantage of Dominique's absence to change her habits, even more so because that absence had been involuntary. Dominique had gone away against her will, and before going her eyes had sent her excuses to the windows opposite.

The Cailles came in. They had seen her light under the door. They whispered, wondering whether they ought to go and greet her and report that all had gone well while she was away, that no one had called except the gas man, and they had not paid because . . .

Lina's voice:

"Perhaps she's undressed."

Then a silence. They were smiling at the idea of their landlady's undressing. Why? What right had they to smile? What did they know about her?

They moved around noisily, thinking they were the only people in the world—they and their sheer delight in living, their thoughtlessness and the pleasures they allowed themselves without thought of the future.

They had paid their rent. But did they know whether they would be able to pay at the end of the month?

"Not tonight, Albert . . . You know we can't . . ."

Imagine a woman saying that to a man!

A taxi? It was stopping farther down the street. It was ten past one. . . . The taxi door banged. No steps were yet audible. Crouching in the corner of the window, Dominique managed to get a glimpse of the taxi, the driver placidly waiting, a woman on her feet, leaning through the door, another face against hers.

They kissed. The taxi went back in the direction of Boulevard Haussmann. Antoinette walked quickly, hunting in her bag for her key and making for the middle of the street to look up and make sure there was no longer any light at her parents'-in-law. It was clear that she was alive again. An atmosphere of joy and love wrapped around her like the fur coat in whose warmth she was snuggling. She slipped into the hallway, hesitated at the elevator, and climbed the stairs on tiptoe.

In her own apartment, she switched on only the bedside lamp. No doubt she let her clothes fall to the floor, just like that, and slipped between the sheets. A few minutes later the pink radiance was gone. There was not a soul stirring in the neighborhood. Dominique was as much alone as old Augustine, who had no one to watch over her motionless corpse.

The same feverish excitement, the same behavior, the same stratagems, the same spurts of gaiety, and the same docility toward Madame Rouet could be seen.

Antoinette, with newfound amiability toward her mother-in-law, would go up without being summoned, would apply herself to trifling tasks, would anticipate the old people's wishes.

The only change was in the time. And the days. Did she still say she was going to her mother's?

At four-thirty, she would go out, reining in her impatience while she walked as far as Saint-Philippe-du-Roule. There she plunged into the first taxi.

"Place Blanche!"

It was a new kind of mystery. The taxi could not get through the crowded streets fast enough, and a gloved hand would be on the door handle even before it had stopped.

A dance hall, with vulgar gilding, mirrors, red hangings, a box office:

ENTRANCE: FIVE FRANCS

An enormous room, tables beyond number, spotlights contrasting with filtered illumination, and in this unreal light a hundred, two hundred, couples slowly revolved, while outside, fifty yards away, the life of the city rolled and broke, like waves, tossing around cars, buses, people carrying things, running God knows where in pursuit of themselves.

An Antoinette transfigured, her mink coat floating behind her, an Antoinette entering this new world as though it were seventh heaven, walked straight to one corner of the room, her hand outstretched, her glove already off. Another hand grasped it, a man half rose, but only half, because she was already at his side, and he was soon stroking the black silk covering her knee.

"Here I am."

One orchestra succeeded another. The spotlights changed from yellow to violet. The couples, after hesitating an instant, began to revolve to a new rhythm, while other couples emerged from dark recesses at the sides.

Thus, at five o'clock each afternoon there were three hundred, perhaps five hundred women there who had escaped from reality. There were as many men, nearly all young, coolly waiting for them, keeping an eye on them, moving warily and silently to and fro, smoking cigarettes.

Antoinette touched up the red on her lips and the slightly yellowish pink on her cheeks. A look asked:

Shall we dance?

And the man slipped his arm under her fur to the warmth generated by her body, his hand resting on flesh rendered smoother by the silk of her dress—smoother and still more supple, more truly flesh than ever, and more feminine. She smiled through half-parted lips, and soon they were lost amid the other couples, seeing nothing but themselves through their half-closed lids.

The man murmured like an incantation:

"Come . . ."

And Antoinette no doubt answered:

"One more . . ."

One more dance . . . To delay the moment of pleasure
. . . To render desire more piercing . . . Perhaps to feel
there, surrounded by other men and women, what Dominique had felt in the train . . .

"Come . . ."

"A little longer . . ."

And their faces showed clearly that they had begun
the act of love.

"Come . . ."

She resisted no longer.

"My bag . . ."

She had been on the point of forgetting it. She let
herself be led, went through the heavy red velvet curtains, felt the coolness of the entryway on her cheeks,
and passed by the glass cage of a box office:

ADMISSION: FIVE FRANCS

The cars and the buses, the lights and the crowd, a
kind of river to ford or to skirt, a street corner to be
turned, and, immediately after a grocery, a threshold to
cross, a black marble slab with gilt letters and a narrow
corridor that smelled of washing.

That day Antoinette paused on the threshold. Her
pupils dilated for a second. She had recognized a black
silhouette, a pale face turned toward her, eyes devouring
her, and her lips curled in a triumphant, disdainful
smile—the smile of a woman letting herself be carried
off on the masterful arm of a male.

The couple sank without trace. . . .

There was nothing left but the beginning of a corridor, people passing the window of a grocery, and the image of the man who had followed Antoinette up the stairs—a mulatto with insolent eyes.

− 9 −

It happened on the twelfth of February. Really, Antoinette had been asking for it for several days, as Dominique had seen. It was not due merely to heedlessness or to bravado: borne along by her passion, carried away by a whirlwind, she hurried consciously to disaster.

However, it did not come through the concierge, nor consequently through Monsieur Rouet, as Dominique had expected. Two days before, she had caught the concierge stopping the landlord, after some hesitation, as he went by. It was doubtless to tell him that a man was entering the building each evening and not leaving until very early the next morning. The concierge knew whose apartment the man went to. She had even been paid to keep quiet; Antoinette had been stupid enough to stop outside the lodge and take a large bill out of her bag.

"I'm sure you'll be discreet, Madame Chochoi!"

But to be sure of others' discretion, you must first display your own, and not let them think you are gaily careering to the abyss. Yet that was the impression Antoinette radiated. Her smile, shining with joy, overflowing with unambiguous happiness, was a provocation. Her laugh resembled the cries that love-making must wring from her, and her sharp teeth seemed always in search of someone to bite. No matter what her dress, her naked body, her gleaming flesh could be sensed beneath it.

The concierge had been afraid for her job and, after consulting her husband, who was night watchman at a chocolate factory, she had informed Monsieur Rouet of what was going on.

He, to Dominique's astonishment, had passed nothing on to his wife. Therefore the latest anonymous note—the third—had misfired, like the earlier ones.

"Be careful!"

Sincerely, naïvely, she had wanted to put Antoinette on her guard and to make her realize that danger hung over her. But Antoinette, as soon as she received the message, had deliberately opened the window, although it was winter, had reread the note ostentatiously, crumpled it into a ball, and thrown it in the fireplace.

What did she think of Dominique? She had recognized her. She knew now that the tenant opposite was the stealthy silhouette of Rue Montaigne and the dance hall area, and that those eyes trained on her from morning till night were the dramatic eyes she had defied as she went into the little hotel on Rue Lepic, next door to the grocery.

A fanatic! Not exactly that, she guessed, but she had other things to do besides trying to probe this mystery.

On the evening of the eleventh of February the mulatto stood as usual in the recess of a doorway, smoking, while he waited for the light to go out in the fourth-floor windows. The Rouets nearly always went to bed at the same hour. There were only a few minutes longer to wait.

Yet that wait was too long, and Antoinette, in her nightgown, felt compelled to draw aside her bedroom curtain and stand there gazing at her lover.

Finally he had rung the bell, the door had opened, and he had gone up. He walked with an offensive litheness, an impudent assurance, which Dominique found unpleasant.

That night the Cailles, too, offended her, without knowing it. After dinner they had come back with a girl who had visited them two or three times before, but during the day. They must have brought back some champagne, for the popping of corks had been heard. They were very cheerful. The phonograph had played nonstop.

It was shocking and depressing to hear Lina's voice growing shriller as she became intoxicated, and eventually she did nothing but laugh and laugh without stopping.

Not once did Dominique look through the keyhole. Nonetheless she sensed the suggestive excitement prevailing next door as she heard Albert's voice pleading again and again:

"Yes, yes! You'll stay. It's late. . . . We'll squeeze you in."

Suddenly he had switched off the light, and Dominique heard them moving around, whispering, and running into one another in the dark. There had been more laughter and feeble protests.

"Have you got enough room?"

The three of them had gone to bed together. Lina had been the first to fall silent, after the inevitable had occurred. Much later, Dominique had realized that the others were not asleep, and she had listened to this secret life, stifled as it was in the sweaty warmth of the bed.

Why had it been a disappointment? At last she had fallen asleep.

A pale sun greeted her in the morning. The sparrows near the Haussmann crossing cheeped in their tree. At eight o'clock Cécile went downstairs, as she did every morning, and opened the third-floor curtains, except in the bedroom, which she never entered until Antoinette rang for her.

Then Dominique saw, at the same time the maid did, that on a little table in the antechamber to the bedroom were a man's gray felt hat and an overcoat.

Antoinette's lover had overslept that morning; it was bound to happen one day.

Her little eyes shining with pleasure, Cécile hurried to the floor above, where old Madame Rouet was not yet on duty in her tower.

"There is a man in madame's bedroom!"

For a few seconds Dominique, without moving, lived through the whole drama. She had time to spare and she saw herself running down to the street and into the coal seller's, where there was a telephone.

"Hello! It's a friend speaking. It doesn't matter who. . . . The maid has seen the hat and the coat. She's gone up to tell Madame Rouet. . . . She'll be coming down in a minute. . . ."

All of that passed through her mind, but she did not stir.

Upstairs, Madame Rouet and her husband were at breakfast. Were they arguing about which one of them should go down?

It was she who went. Her husband remained upstairs. That morning he was not seen leaving the house for his unvarying walk to Rue Coquillière.

"You'd better stay . . . in case . . ."

Dominique saw Madame Rouet, leaning on her cane, enter the antechamber and sit down in a chair Cécile pushed forward for her.

Were the two still asleep, or had they heard? Never had Madame Rouet been so still or so menacing. Her calm was colossal. It was as though she were living at last, down to the smallest crumb, the hour for which she had been preparing for years.

She had waited, confident that this hour would come. For months past, every day, at every meal, every time Antoinette came up, she had stared at her as if to assure herself that the moment was not far off now.

At half past eight, at quarter to nine, there was no movement. Only at ten minutes before nine was the bedroom curtain moved slightly, then fully opened, and Dominique was able to see Antoinette, who obviously knew she was caught in a trap.

She had not dared ring for her maid. She didn't dare open the bedroom door either. She bent down to the keyhole; through it she could undoubtedly see the chair on which her mother-in-law sat, on guard.

The man was sitting on the edge of the bed, anxious, perhaps, but impudent even so. And she jerked out nervously:

"Come on, get dressed! What are you waiting for?"

As he dressed, he smoked his first cigarette.

"Stay there. Don't budge . . . No! . . . Go into the bathroom. Keep calm . . ."

Then, in her dressing gown, its wide sleeves floating

out, with her feet in blue satin mules, Antoinette took a deep breath and opened the door.

They were face to face. Old Madame Rouet did not flinch, did not look at her daughter-in-law, but continued staring at the hat and coat on the little table.

Without a moment's thought, Antoinette sprang violently to the attack.

"What are you doing here? . . . Answer me! You forget that this is my apartment. . . . It's still mine, whatever you may think. . . . I order you to go! Do you hear? This is my home, *mine*, and I'm entitled to do what I like here."

Facing her was a block of marble, a statue leaning on a rubber-tipped cane, a look of ice.

Antoinette, unable to stand still, walked up and down, the skirts of her dressing gown sailing around her. She was surely restraining herself from breaking some ornament or hurling herself on her enemy.

"I order you to leave. . . . Can't you hear? . . . I've had enough! Yes, I've had enough of you, of your pretenses, of your family, of your apartments. I've had enough of . . ."

The man had left the bathroom door open, and Dominique could see him listening, and still smoking.

Not for a second did Madame Rouet's lips move. She had nothing to say. The corners of her mouth, however, turned down in a sign of deeper scorn, of unutterable disgust, as Antoinette desperately continued screaming.

What need was there to hear the words? The gestures told quite enough, the hair flying in all directions, the heaving bosom.

"What are you waiting for? . . . To find out whether

I have a lover? . . . Well, I have. A man! A real man; not a miserable specimen like your son. . . . Do you want to see him? Is that what you're waiting for? . . . Pierre! Pierre!"

The man did not budge.

"Come on! Let my mother-in-law take a good look at you! . . . Now are you satisfied? . . . Oh, I know what you're going to say: You own the apartment. What don't you own? . . . I'll go, of course. But not before I've told you what I think, not before I've had my say . . . Yes, I have a lover. But you and your family, your frightful family, you're . . ."

Dominique was pale. For a second, as she strode vehemently to and fro, Antoinette's eye fell on her and she paused, appearing satisfied to be seen at that moment. She sneered and screamed louder, while her lover moved toward the door. Madame Rouet still did not budge. She was waiting for it to be over, for the apartment to be empty at last.

For a full half-hour Antoinette continued her agitated pacing while she dressed, going in and out of her bedroom, yelling sometimes at the man and sometimes at her mother-in-law.

"I'm going, but . . ."

She was ready at last. She had put on her mink coat, the richness of which was belied by her intentional vulgarity.

She reached the door, screamed another insult, and took her companion's arm, but then she retraced her steps to spit out a coarse phrase at Cécile, standing at the pantry door, whom she had overlooked.

The street was quiet, and the light was soft. Looking

down, Dominique saw the couple leave the building and look for a taxi. It was Antoinette who spoke to the driver, apparently taking charge of her companion.

As for Madame Rouet, she turned to Cécile and said:

"Shut the door . . . No; first go and get the master. . . ."

He came down. A couple of sentences, no more, told him all. Madame Rouet got up painfully from the chair and then, for nearly an hour, she inspected the furniture and the drawers, collecting things that had belonged to her son. She was to be seen holding a watch and chain, photographs, cuff links, a silver fountain pen, and various trifles of no value.

She handed her finds to her husband.

"She'll be back. If I know her, she's gone to her mother's. Her mother will think about practical matters at once. Very soon they'll come back to get everything. . . ."

She was quite right. At Place Blanche, the taxi stopped. The lover got out into the reassuring coolness of a familiar scene and made his way, at a relaxed pace, to a bar.

"I'll telephone you. . . ."

The taxi climbed Rue Caulaincourt. Antoinette's mother, a scarf around her graying hair, was cleaning her room, making a fine cloud of luminous dust.

"Well, that's it!"

Despair. Anxiety.

"*Why* did you do it?"

"Oh, Mama, no sermons, please. I've had enough! I've had enough to drown me. . . ."

"You've not called your sister? Perhaps you ought to ask her advice. . . ."

Young Colette, of the lips with the candid upward curve, of the innocent and heartrending smile, was the family's business head.

"Hello . . . Yes . . . What do you say? . . . Do you think so? . . . Yes, they're capable of that. Wait; I'll make a note. A pencil, please, Mama . . . Papin. Evaluator. What street? . . . All right, I've got it. Thank you . . . I don't know yet when . . . No, not at Mama's. In the first place, there isn't room. . . . Later . . . Yes, of course! . . . That's it. . . . The stage I've reached . . ."

There was loud laughter from the Cailles'. Lina had a hangover and thought she was ill. This made her fretful and angry.

"You're making fun of me. I know you're making fun of me. . . . I was too hot all night. Neither of you stopped kicking. . . ."

Across the street, Cécile had opened all the windows, as if the apartment was empty already.

At eleven o'clock a taxi pulled up. Antoinette got out, accompanied by her mother and a badly dressed man who looked the building up and down, as if to draw up its inventory. Behind them came an aggressively yellow moving van.

There was no question of lunch. In the course of three hours a clean sweep was made of the rooms. Furniture was dismantled, the evaluator noted down everything that crossed the threshold, and Antoinette seemed to be secretly enjoying the sight of the furniture leaving piece by piece, the hangings disappearing from windows and doors, and the parquet floor showing gray where the carpets had been taken up.

Like a ferret, she went around making sure nothing had been left. It was she who thought of wine for the moving men and went to the cellar. It was she, too, who noticed that certain objects were missing and, calling to the evaluator, dictated a list, pointing to the ceiling, accusing her mother-in-law.

A whole life was being trampled on, pillaged, annihilated in one morning, with great, swift strokes, with sadistic joy.

She brought such intensity to the job that her mother, who did not know what to do with herself, was apparently frightened; and, at her window, Dominique's heart was wrung.

Dominique did not eat either. She was not hungry, and she lacked the will to go down and do her shopping.

The Cailles went out. A ray of sunshine had brought thoughts of spring, and Lina put on a light-colored suit and sported a little red hat. Albert, extremely happy and proud, walked between her and the girl who had spent the night in their bed.

Mademoiselle Augustine's room had not yet been rented. It was only a servant's room, too far away from the street. Another old maid would have to be found to live in it, but they had not bothered to put up a sign, the concierge having thought it sufficient to tell the local tradesmen.

At the curb a second van succeeded the first. Madame Rouet, in her tower, could hear the turmoil below her. When the place was quite empty at last, when there was nothing left—not a piece of furniture, not a carpet, not a curtain, not, above all, a living soul—she would go down in triumph to survey the field of battle.

At two o'clock Colette got out of a taxi and went upstairs. She kissed her sister and her mother, but showed no emotion and little interest. She simply pointed to a chromium-plated standing lamp, and Antoinette shrugged her shoulders.

"Take it if you like!"

Later, was it Antoinette who gave the order? Or did the moving men take them with the rest of the things from the back room where they had been put? Anyway, Dominique saw a workman cross the sidewalk carrying two green plants in pots. They, too, disappeared into the crowded van.

There was one mistake. A dark green coat had been carried off with a jumble of other garments, and Cécile went down to get it, because it belonged to her. From a fourth-floor window she had seen it in the arms of one of the men; or perhaps she had been mounting guard in the hall.

By five o'clock it was all finished. Antoinette had made several telephone calls. She had drunk a glass of wine from one of the moving men's bottles, using one of their glasses after rinsing it out.

When all of them had gone, the only things left in the apartment were bottles, one of them half full, and dirty glasses set down on the floor.

Antoinette had forgotten her neighbor of the window opposite. Not a glance by way of farewell. It was only down below, on the sidewalk, that she remembered her and looked up, and her lips curled in a mocking smile.

"Good-bye, my dear! I'm getting out of . . ."

The evaluator had departed with his papers. He had arrived by taxi, but went off by bus, for which he had a long wait at the corner of Boulevard Haussmann, near the tree where the birds lived.

"Aren't you hungry?" asked Antoinette's mother as they drove along.

She was always hungry. She loved everything eatable, but especially lobster, foie gras, rich sauces and pastries.

Wasn't now the time, if ever, for eating?

"No, Mama. I must . . ."

She did not take her mother back to her apartment. She dropped her at Place Clichy, slipping some money into her hand by way of consolation.

"Don't fuss . . . Of course I'll come and see you to-morrow. . . . No, not in the morning . . . Don't you understand anything? . . . Take me to Graff's, driver."

She condescended to wave a hand through the window. At Graff's she immediately picked out the man, who was waiting for her with a drink in front of him.

"Now let's go and have dinner . . . Are you pleased? . . . Ooh! I can't feel my legs any more. Heavens, what a day! . . . What's the matter? Are you upset? . . . Mama wanted me to move in with her, while I'm looking for a small place. . . . I've had everything put in storage. . . . Waiter, a port! . . . My bag has been taken to your hotel."

They ate dinner in an Italian restaurant on Boulevard Rochechouart. The sudden calm, the silence that surrounded them, unsettled Antoinette, and now and then anxiety, perhaps foreboding, betrayed itself in the covert glances she darted at her lover.

"Listen. Tonight, to celebrate my freedom, I'd like . . ."

They celebrated it in every dance hall they could find; and the more champagne she drank the more excited Antoinette became and the shriller her voice grew. She had to let herself go. If she remained still for a moment, she became upset, wild distress gripped her. She laughed, she danced, she talked at the top of her voice. She had to be the center of attraction and deliberately created scenes. At four in the morning they were the last customers in a little nightclub on Rue Fontaine. She was weeping on the mulatto's shoulder like a little girl, whining, melting with pity for herself and for him.

"*You* understand, at least? . . . Tell me you understand . . . There's only us two left now, you see. There's nothing else. . . . Tell me there's nothing but us two. Kiss me, hold me tight . . ."

"The waiter's looking at us."

She insisted on trying to drink one more bottle, but she knocked it over. Her mink was thrown over her shoulders. When she stumbled on the curb, the man put his arm around her waist to hold her up. Suddenly, near a lamp, she leaned over and was sick. Tears, but not from weeping, started from her eyes as she tried to laugh once more and repeated:

"It's nothing. . . . It's nothing. . . ."

Then, clinging to her lover, who kept his head turned away, she whined:

"I don't disgust you, do I? Swear that I don't disgust you, that I will never disgust you. . . . Because now, you know . . ."

He helped her, one step at a time, up the stairs in the Hotel Beauséjour, on Rue Notre-Dame-de-Lorette, where he rented a bedroom and bath by the week.

On Rue du Faubourg Saint-Honoré the windows remained open on emptiness all night, and Dominique's first sensation on waking in the morning was of the emptiness opposite, with which she must now live.

Then there came back to her a forgotten memory— a memory of the time when she was a little girl, a time when her mother and her father, the General, were moving, transferring from one garrison to another. They used to move often, and each time, when she saw the house being emptied, she kept as close as possible to the front door, for fear of being overlooked.

Antoinette had not overlooked her, since she *had* glanced up at the last moment.

She had gone, and she had left Dominique behind on purpose.

Dominique lighted the gas mechanically, to warm her coffee, and she thought of old Mademoiselle Augustine, who had also gone, but had run after the train to come and, still panting, tell her of the joy of her deliverance.

— 10 —

The day began like any other, with nothing to suggest that it would be out of the ordinary. Far otherwise. The air was so clear and mild, and Dominique was so much in tune with the dawn, that there seemed to be good hope of recovery.

It was the third of March, though she was unaware of this. She had forgotten to tear the leaf off the calendar. It was not yet spring, but she could now open her window wide in the morning, while shutters elsewhere were still closed, and wait for the songs of the birds to join the sound of the fountain at the old mansion nearby. The fresh, slightly damp morning air had a tang that recalled the vegetable-filled marketplace of some little town, and, early in the season though it was, aroused in her a longing for fruit.

She thought of plums that morning. This evoked a memory of childhood, of a town she had lived in—she could not remember which—a marketplace she'd crossed with her father in full uniform. She was in her Sunday best, a white frock stiff with starch. The General

171

was leading her by the hand. His saber glinted in the sun close to her eyes. Walls of plums in baskets extended on both sides of the street. The air smelled so strongly of plums that the scent followed them into the church, the doors of which were left open for the Te Deum. There were a great many flags. Men in civilian clothes were wearing arm bands.

It was odd, but recently she would be seized at any moment by a childhood memory and sink happily into it. Sometimes, as on this morning, she would even think in the same way as when she was a little girl. For example, the sun was rising a little earlier each morning and each evening the lights had to be put on a little later, and Dominique said to herself, as if announcing a certainty:

"When we can have dinner in the evening without the lights on, I shall be saved!"

That had once been her idea of the way the year went. There were the months, long and dark as a tunnel, during which you sat at the table under the lighted lamp, and the months during which you could walk in the garden after the evening meal.

Her mother, who used to think that each winter would be her last, did not think of it in quite the same way. For her, it was the month of May that constituted the critical stage.

"Soon May will be here, and things will be better."

So on this morning, as on others, she lived half in the reality of the present, half among the memories of other days. She saw the empty apartment opposite, still not rented, a touch of pink on the housefronts, a for-gotten geranium in a pot on Mademoiselle Augustine's windowsill. She heard the early noises of the street, and inhaled a passing whiff of coffee. But at the same time she thought she could catch bugle calls, the noises her father made getting up in the morning, his spurs jingling in the hallway, the bang of the door he could never learn to shut quietly. A quarter of an hour before the General left, his horse could be heard in front of that same door, pawing the ground while an orderly held its bridle.

She was filled with melancholy because all the recollections were very old—all, without exception, from before her sixteenth birthday, as if only the early years had counted, as if the rest had been merely a long succession of empty days that had left nothing behind.

Was life just that? A brief, unconscious childhood, a short adolescence, then emptiness, tangles of troubles, worries, and trivial cares, and then, so soon, at forty, the feeling of being old, of a slope to be descended without happiness or joy?

The Cailles were leaving her. They were going on the fifteenth of March. It was not Albert who had given her this news. He knew it would cause her pain and he was too much of a coward to do that to her. He had sent Lina. They had whispered together, as always in such circumstances. He had pushed her toward the door, and Lina, as she came in, had looked more than ever like a pink doll stuffed with bran, or a little schoolgirl who has forgotten her recitation.

"I must tell you, Madam Salès . . . now that my husband is contributing regularly to a paper, he needs an office, perhaps a secretary. . . . We've been hunting for an apartment, and we've found one on Quai Voltaire, with windows looking out on the Seine. We move in on the fifteenth of March. . . . We'll always have the happiest recollections of our stay with you and of all your many kindnesses. . . ."

They now got up earlier and went busily around the city, setting up their new place, excited and radiant, and coming back only to sleep, as if in a hotel room. Sometimes they didn't come back at all, but doubtless spent the night on a mattress in their new home.

Dominique moved around her room, performing the same actions, one after another; and morning was, in truth, the best part of her day, because there was a long-established rhythm to carry her along.

She looked at the time on the little watch hanging in its silk slipper. Her mother's gold watch, ornamented with brilliants, made her think of the calendar, and she tore off the leaf of the day before, to uncover the great black figure 3.

It was the anniversary of her mother's death. That year, too, she had talked of the month of May as the haven she hoped to reach, but she had been seized by suffocation toward the end of a wet day.

Dominique could think of her mother now without regret. She could picture her quite well, though not in detail. She saw a fragile shape, a long face always bent slightly forward, a being whose flame always burned low, as it were. She was not touched, but called up the picture coldly, perhaps with a little resentment. This incapacity, so to speak, for living—because she fully realized that she was impotent in the face of life—had been instilled in her by her mother, along with elegant resignation, refined self-effacement, and acceptance of trivial activity to relieve loneliness.

She saw Monsieur Rouet leaving as she looked out at the sky, which was clear and bright, but in which she could sense a kind of false promise.

The fine weather was not the kind to last all day. The

yellow of the sun was too pale, the blue was false, and the white of the clouds harbored shadows of rain.

Toward midday, she knew instinctively, the sky would be entirely overcast, and long before dinnertime there would descend on the city that distressing twilight that drifts through the streets like mysterious dust.

Nervous and uneasy, she felt the urge, God knows why, to do her spring-cleaning; and she got through a good part of the day at close quarters with buckets of water, brushes, and dustrags. By three o'clock she had nearly finished polishing the furniture.

She already knew what was going to happen—at least what was going to happen very soon.

When there was nothing left for her to do, when, with a ritual gesture, she set the stocking basket on the table, when the light began to turn a dull gray, she would be seized by an anguish she knew only too well.

Did the same sort of thing happen to Monsieur Rouet, in his strange office on Rue Coquillière? And the summons was more peremptory on rainy days, when evening fell more quickly and uncertain light gave the streets a different look.

He, too, was doubtless trying to resist, crossing and uncrossing his legs, mastering the trembling of his fingers. He, too, would get up, shamefaced, and say in a voice not quite his own:

"I must go to the bank, Bronstein. . . . If my wife telephones . . ."

He would slip down the stairs. Seized with giddiness, he would make his way toward the narrowest, dirtiest streets, where shadowy corners reeked of vice. And there he would edge along damp walls.

She poured herself a cup of coffee and buttered a

slice of bread, as if that was going to hold her back. She had scarcely sat down again and was about to put the varnished wooden egg into a stocking, when the summons became irresistible. She put on her coat and hat, taking care not to look at her reflection in the mirror.

On the stairs she wondered whether she'd locked her door. At any other time she would have gone back to check. Why not today?

She waited for the bus, then stood on the back platform among the hard forms of men smelling of tobacco. But *it* had not yet begun, *it* would only begin much farther on, in accordance with rules that never varied.

She got out at the Place Clichy. It was not yet raining, though there was a veil around the lamps, a halo in front of lighted shop windows. All at once, she entered a new life, where huge lighted signs were the guiding marks.

Ten times, perhaps more often, she had gone out this way, her nerves taut, and each time she had hurried along not knowing where she was going. She had constantly wanted to stop, and out of shame had pretended not to see anything around her. Yet, like a thief, she had gulped in the life flowing by her on every side.

Ten times she had fled her room, so still at this hour that the stillness weighed on her agonizingly. Two or three times she had gone like this to the neighborhood of the markets, into those alleys where she had followed Monsieur Rouet, but most often she came here to prowl with the hungry eyes of a beggar.

Furtive, conscious of her shame, she rubbed shoulders with the crowd, sniffing its odor. Without her realizing it, the ritual had become established. She always crossed the place at the same spot, went around a certain corner, recognized the smell of certain little bars and shops, hesitated at a particular crossing where the scent was stronger than elsewhere.

She was feeling so wretched that she could have whimpered as she walked. She was alone, more alone than anyone. What would happen if she were to fall down in the gutter? A passerby would stumble over her body. A few people would stop. She would be carried into a shop, and a policeman would remove the elastic band from his notebook.

"Who is it?"

No one would know.

Would she see Antoinette again today? She had found her, finally. It was in search of her that, the first few times, she had come to wander around this neighborhood.

But why did her eyes burrow deep into all those warm mouths, the entrances of hotels? By some of these, women waited. Dominique would rather not have looked at them, but the urge was too strong for her. Some were tired, their patience almost gone: others looked her calmly in the eyes, seeming to say:

"What does *she* want?"

It soon seemed to Dominique that she could recognize, by their walk, by something stealthy and embarrassed about them, the men whom desire was driving toward one of those entrances. They would brush close to her. Sometimes, in the darkness between two shop windows or two street lamps one of them leaned over her to see her face. And she had not been shocked. She had been unable to feel shocked. She had shivered and walked on for a minute or two seeing nothing, as though her eyes were shut.

She was alone. Antoinette treated her with scorn. It had happened once. It might happen again today.

Some evenings, Dominique saw her sitting alone in a bar on the Place Blanche, jumping every time the door opened or the telephone rang.

He would not come. Or else he kept her waiting for hours. She would buy an evening paper, open her bag, take out her compact and lipstick. Her eyes had changed. Though the same excitement haunted them, it was tinged now with anxiety, perhaps even weariness.

But today he was there. There were four of them around a table, two men and two women. Exactly like that evening when Antoinette had nudged her lover's elbow and drawn his attention to the window with a jerk of her chin.

"Look!"

It was Dominique she'd been indicating to her companions, Dominique with her face almost glued to the glass before she'd disappeared into the blackness of the street.

Why did Antoinette now have fits of vulgar laughter, quivering with defiance? And that anxiety, terror almost, when she looked at this man who was playing so coolly with her.

Had he threatened to leave her? Was he running after other women? Had he left her alone for whole nights in their room in the Hotel Beauséjour?

Dominique could guess, could feel all that, and she was driven by an urge to bear her part of it. Had not Antoinette gone down on her knees in front of him, bare-breasted and half-naked, groveling at his feet? Had she not savagely threatened to kill him?

Sure of himself, contemptuous and sardonic, he had

complete mastery over her. That was clear from his every look and gesture, still clearer when he looked at his watch—a new wristwatch she had given him—and got up, putting a gray felt hat carefully on his curly hair.

"See you later. You know where. . . ."

"You won't be too late?"

His fingers touched those of his comrade, the two men exchanged a wink, he tapped the other girl on the shoulder, and a pathetic look followed him to the door. Then Antoinette tried to hide her anxiety by renewing her make-up.

It would not last forever. Not even for years. A few months longer?

Perhaps she would not kill him.

And then, a panting she-animal, she would howl her pain and hate, following him in wild pursuit, only to be stopped at the entrances to cafés and dance halls, by waiters or doormen who had been warned against her.

Did she see Dominique that evening? The man friend suggested a game, to calm her after her lover left. He called to the waiter for a cloth and cards, making room on the marble tabletop by pushing aside glasses filled with a greenish apéritif.

Dominique was on the move again, brushing her shoulders against the walls, repelling the ever-recurring memory of two rows of plums and a Te Deum welling through wide-open cathedral doors.

Her apartment on Faubourg Saint-Honoré was empty, utterly empty. Her single log would have gone out long since and there would not be a thing stirring. There would be nothing but chilly air to welcome her home.

Even the women she saw standing at hotel doors must

be less lonely, even the men hesitating before approaching them.

Everything around her was alive, but in her there was only her heart, beating uselessly, like an alarm clock forgotten in a suitcase.

A few weeks more, and the sun would be shining at that time of day. . . . Night would not fall till later, after dinner, bringing peace. . . .

Where was she? A short while before, she had seen the windows of the Hotel Beauséjour; now she was going down a dark, sloping street with no buses or cars. She looked at a cobbler in his little shop. She brushed against a shadow she had failed to see, and the head turned toward her. She was frightened. Her fear increased so suddenly that she wanted to scream. Someone had come up to her, someone she could not clearly see was walking in step with her, someone was touching her—a hand, a man's hand, was gripping her arm. She was being spoken to, though she could not understand the words. All her blood had ebbed, and she was defenseless. She knew— she saw clearly—what was happening to her. What was extraordinary was that she seemed to have accepted it in advance.

Had she always known that someday she would walk, in the darkness of an unknown street, in step with a strange man? Had she lived it in a dream? Or did it come only from having witnessed the same thing, from having followed Antoinette, from having stared wide-eyed as the two shapes, with one and the same movement, plunged into the dim light of a corridor?

She felt no astonishment. She was submissive. She did not dare look at the man, but she noted the strong smell of a cigar that had gone out.

Soon she had crossed a threshold. On the right was a round window; behind it, someone in shirtsleeves, a blue coffeepot on a gas ring.

What had he said? He had reached out a hairy arm and handed over a key, which she had not taken. Yet she was now on the stairs, she was climbing; she must have stopped breathing, and her heart must have stopped beating. There was carpet beneath her feet, a night-light. She felt warm breath; a hand—the hand—touched her again and moved up her leg, reaching the naked flesh above her stocking.

As she reached the next floor, quite out of breath, she turned. She saw first a bowler hat and a middle-aged man's commonplace features. He was smiling. He had a reddish mustache. Then the smile was wiped out, and she knew that he was as astonished as she was. She went rigid, before pushing him back with both hands to force a passage down the stairs he was blocking with his bulk. She ran, ran at fantastic speed, it seemed to her. The street seemed very far away, and she thought she would never reach the sidewalk, the lighted shops, the comforting buses.

When she did stop, she found herself just outside the Gare Saint-Lazare. The throng was at its thickest, because all the clerks and other workers of Paris were rushing to catch their suburban trains.

Mechanically, she glanced behind her once more, but she had not been followed. She was alone, quite alone, though jostled by the hurrying crowds.

Half-aloud, she stammered:

"It's all over."

She could not have said what was all over. Empty, hollow, she started walking again. The taste of stale cigar was in her mouth, and the smell of those hotel stairs clung to her. And the picture of that lobby, where in the gloom she had caught a glimpse of an apathetic chambermaid's white apron.

So that was how it was!

Poor Nique!

She was clearheaded, terribly clearheaded.

Yes, it was all over. What was the use? There wasn't even any need to hurry. It was all over, quite over! And how little it had amounted to! You imagine that life . . .

"Spring term"—yet another phrase from her childhood. They used to talk of the spring term as a period that would never come to an end. . . . The term before the Easter holidays . . .

For quite a long time, the days never finish and the weeks are an eternity, with Sunday's sun far away at the end, and then suddenly nothing is left—just months and years made up of hours and days all jumbled together in confusion, with nothing standing out at all.

It's all over. . . .

She might well feel pity for herself. It *was* all over.

It's all over, poor Nique.

You didn't do it. You will never do it. You won't live to be a poor old maid like Mademoiselle Augustine either. . . .

It's too bad Antoinette didn't look at you today!

Well-known sidewalks, Audebal's dairy, Sutton's luggage, for people going on long journeys.

A little farther up the street was a flower shop, and Dominique went to it past her own building. Rain had begun to fall, and the drops made long diagonal streaks across the window.

"Give me some . . ."

She would have liked daisies. The word had sprung naturally to her lips, but as she looked around, she could not see any daisies like those she used to arrange in a vase while she thought of Jacques Améraud.

"Some what, madame?"

. . . Jacques Améraud . . . Old Madame Améraud, who . . .

"Roses . . . A lot of roses."

If only she had enough money with her. She paid. It was the last time she would count out bills and coins.

If only the Cailles were still out. She bore them no ill-will, but they had hurt her. They were not responsible. They were going their own way. They thought they were getting somewhere. . . .

Was it just for the sake of speaking once more to a human being that she pushed open the lodge door?

"Nothing for me?"

"No, madame."

She had not remembered that she had the roses. The concierge looked at them in astonishment, and Dominique smiled apologetically, a very gentle smile.

She *was* gentle; that was her character, the character her mother had formed for her. She made no noise on the stairs. She had been taught to go upstairs quietly, not to disturb people, to keep out of the way. . . .

To keep out of the way! From what a distance that expression came back to her! That was indeed it. She had kept out of the way. Now she was going to go even farther out of the way. . . .

Before drawing the curtains, Dominique took a last look at the windows opposite. She raised her head a little and saw old Madame Rouet in her tower.

The tower mounts guard. . . .

Her eyes grew wet. She turned on the light and looked at herself, standing before the mirror.

Still, she was not an old maid yet.

She unbuttoned her dress. The mirror disappeared when she opened the wardrobe. She still possessed a long nightdress trimmed with Valenciennes lace, a nightdress she had worked on for three months once upon a time.

"For when you get married . . ."

She still had a bottle of amber-colored eau de cologne in a drawer.

She gave a wry little smile as she hurried, because she felt a premonition of revolt springing up inside. She was beginning to wonder whether somebody was not responsible for . . .

The bottle . . . where was the bottle? She had bought it three years earlier, when migraines were keeping her awake all night. . . . She had taken a tablet only once.

Well! She had done her spring-cleaning that very morning. The room smelled clean. The furniture was gleaming. She counted the tablets as she dropped them into a glass of water: eight . . . nine . . . ten . . . eleven . . .

Would that be enough?

Yet, if she wanted . . . if . . .

No! Not now.

"Oh, God, I beg . . . grant that . . ."

She drank and lay down. Her chest felt rather tight, because of the bitterness of the medicine. She had sprinkled eau de cologne over the bed, and, lying down, she arranged the roses around her.

When one of her little schoolmates had died, she had

been surrounded by flowers. The mothers had said through their tears:

"She looks like an angel!"

Was the drug working already? She did not stir, did not feel the slightest desire to stir—she who had always had a horror of lying in bed. She heard all the noises of the street, waited for the clatter of buses, the grinding noise they made changing gear at the foot of the hill. She wanted to hear once more the ringing of the bell in Audebal's shop.

Why, she had forgotten something! She had forgotten the one thing that mattered, and now it was too late!

Antoinette would not know.

She would so much have liked . . . What would she so much have liked? What was she thinking of? . . . She felt ill. . . . No; it was only that her tongue was becoming bigger, was swelling inside her mouth, but it did not matter, it did not hurt. . . .

"It doesn't hurt, darling."

Who used to say that? . . . Her mother? Yes, her mother, when she had skinned a knee and iodine was being put on . . .

No; it didn't hurt. . . . Had it hurt Jacques Améraud? . . .

Where had she been? . . . She had been to look for something, somewhere, very far away. . . . Yes, it was already very far away. . . . Had she found . . . ?

She could not tell any more. . . . It was ridiculous that she could not tell any more. The whole family would be very surprised. In Toulon, she had felt no love for them. . . . What was it they had done to her again? She had forgotten. Perhaps it was because they had gone off

185

and left her all alone. . . . They did not seem to see her. The proof was the way they said:

"You haven't changed, Nique!"

Who was calling her Nique? She was alone. She had always been alone.

Perhaps if she were given sixteen drops of the medicine on the bedside table . . . Why did Antoinette stay behind the door, instead of going in to pour out the drops?

You're a little fool, Nique! You know you've always been told you were a little fool. With all your grand notions, you used to forget the one thing that mattered. . . . Now, you forgot to warn Antoinette. . . . She's way up there in the café. She's playing a game of cards. . . .

You even forgot that the roses would smell bad. Flowers always smell bad in a room with a dead body.

When the Cailles come in . . . They won't know. They'll think the place is the same as ever. . . . Perhaps they'll just remark that they don't hear you scurrying around like a mouse, as you usually do. But that'll be all the same to them. They'll undress, they'll cling to each other, and sighs will be heard. . . .

There'll be no one to hear them. . . . In the morning, perhaps . . .

Albert Caille will be frightened. They'll whisper together. He'll say to Lina:

"Go on, you go!"

He'll give her a push.

It was a dirty trick to play on them, especially since they have less than a fortnight left to live here. They won't even know whom they should send telegrams to.

The family will all be obliged to catch trains, from

186

Rennes, from Toulon, from Angoulême. Luckily, they'll still have their mourning clothes!

"To think that the last time we saw her, at Aunt Clémentine's funeral, she looked so . . ."

"I thought she looked just a little bit unhappy."

Why? It was not true. She had never been unhappy. She had kept her promise, that was all. Soon she must hurry to tell Antoinette.

It would be easy. . . . In a few minutes, in a few seconds, it would all be over, and she would do what Mademoiselle Augustine had done. She would hurry to Antoinette's side and cry out to her, quivering with joy:

"See! I've come. It was you I wanted to see first of all. Do you understand? . . . I couldn't tell you, before. I used to look at you from a long way off, and you didn't understand. . . . Now that it's all over . . ."

She blushed. . . . Was she still capable of blushing? She was in a muddle. A cold shiver gripped her whole body. . . .

Yes, a few seconds yet. Four, three, two . . . not more. Very soon now she would be clasping Antoinette in her arms, leaning over her face, over those lips that were so alive, so alive . . .

So . . .

"Don't worry about Pierre, my dear. So long as he said he'd come, he'll come."

Antoinette did her best to smile. It was midnight. She had been left alone in a corner of a bar. Catching sight of herself in a mirror, she thought she looked like a woman waiting for just anybody.

187

Monsieur Rouet got up from his armchair and went to undress, while his wife, leaning on her cane, straightened the living room.

She had telephoned to Rue Coquillière, and he had not been there. She was waiting for him to go to sleep so she could count the money in his wallet. As though he did not know and did not take precautions!

He had borrowed a hundred francs from Bronstein.

He had worked so hard all his life to earn his money.

He had had no luck today. When the little trollop had undressed and lain down on the red bedcover, he had seen tiny spots all along her thin thighs, and, frightened, he had left her.

There was no sound now in Dominique's apartment but the ticking of the alarm clock. When the Cailles came in at last, they did not notice. They undressed and went to bed, but they were too tired after a day spent papering their future home.

She just said, in the voice of one asleep already:

"Not tonight . . ."

He did not insist. Minutes passed.

"About the thousand francs' key money: I think if we were to ask . . ."

Lina was asleep.

The rain fell softly, soundlessly.